The Wife of Bath's Tale
from Chaucer's Canterbury Tales

Geoffrey Chaucer

Edited and translated into modern English by
Dr Simon D Pratt

COLLEGE EDITION
Printed in a larger typeface and with wide margins

The Wife of Bath's Tale
By Geoffrey Chaucer
Edited and translated by Dr Simon D Pratt

First published in 2018 by McGowan Publications, 244 Madison Avenue, 10016-287, New York City, USA.

This revised Schools and Colleges edition is published by Simon D Pratt - who may be contacted at drsimonpratt@hotmail.com.

ISBN 9798374871555

Translator's Preface

Written between 1387 and 1400, Chaucer's Canterbury Tales is set on a journey made by thirty-one pilgrims (including Chaucer and the host, Harry Bailey) as they travel from Southwark in London to Thomas Becket's shrine at Canterbury. There, in return for the prize of a free dinner, the pilgrims all agreed to participate in a story-telling contest to help make their long journey more enjoyable.

This book contains probably the most favourite tale - that of the Wife of Bath. However, despite its reputation for some lewdness, this prologue and tale provides an important and serious comment on women's lives in early modern England and which, regretfully, casts dark shadows into our twenty-first century lives. For this reason, there is much to be gained from reading Chaucer's fascinating glimpse into a new world that had just started to emerge from the Black Death and the decline of feudal servitude. Nevertheless, to maintain appropriate standards of decorum, the translator has substituted more acceptable -and indirect - terms for the vulgar references sometimes made to genitalia and sexual acts.

This book has been designed to meet readers' needs in three particular ways: Firstly, to present Chaucer's Tale in a larger font size on cream paper that makes the text more accessible to those who may experience reading difficulties, such as dyslexia. Secondly, there are wide margins for writing notes or further explanations. Thirdly, and perhaps most importantly, the side-by-side translation contained in this book is based upon a literal word-for-word approach. Here, readers will find each translated line is placed opposite to the counterpart original text.As a result, the meaning of unfamiliar words can be checked immediately - thereby making the present version particularly useful for those who are new to Middle English. However, there are some instances when this approach might not provide the reader with a clear understanding. In these situations, an explanatory word or phrase is then added to the translation - but these additions are clearly identified by being contained within square brackets [ ].

Many translations of the Canterbury Tales make great efforts to retain the iambic pentameter and rhyming couplet structure of the original text. In many ways, that is a highly laudable endeavour. However, several modern translations have preserved that poetic framework only at the cost of inserting substitute words and phrases which may change the original meaning. Accordingly, the present translation follows a different route that seeks to describe and explain Chaucer's words accurately, but without being held hostage to a poetic format. For this reason, the following translation reflects the renowned 'Riverside Chaucer' version where some lines rhyme, whilst others do not. In any event, the creation of a predominantly non-rhyming version of the Canterbury Tales is not quite so seditious as might first appear. The reader is reminded that Chaucer wrote his Canterbury Tales before the Great Vowel Shift of 1400 to 1600. As a result, the evolution of English pronunciation suggests the Canterbury Tales may already have started to lose its poetic resonance soon after it was written.

Simon D Pratt

The translator was educated at St Chad's College Durham, Warwick, Exeter, De Montfort, and Hull Universities in the United Kingdom having previously been a Hardwicke and Sir Thomas More scholar of the Honourable Society of Lincoln's Inn, London. His publications include works on medieval English law and literature.

The Wife of Bath on horseback

The Wife of Bath's Prologue and Tale

The Prologe of the Wyves Tale of Bathe

Experience, though noon auctoritee

Were in this world, were right ynogh to me

To speke of wo that is in mariage;

For, lordynges, sith I twelf yeer was of age,

5   Thonked be God, that is eterne on lyve,

Housbondes at chirche dore I have had fyve -

For I so ofte have ywedded bee -

And alle were worthy men in hir degree.

But me was toold, certeyn, nat longe agoon is,

10   That sith that Crist ne wente nevere but onis

To weddyng in the Cane of Galilee,

That by the same ensample, taughte he me,

That I ne sholde wedded be but ones.

Herkne eek, lo, which a sharpe word for the nones,

15   Biside a welle Jhesus, God and Man,

Spak in repreeve of the Samaritan.

"Thou hast yhad fyve housbondes," quod he,

"And thilke man the which that hath now thee

Is noght thyn housbonde;" thus seyde he certeyn.

20   What that he mente ther by, I kan nat seyn;

But that I axe, why that the fifthe man

Was noon housbonde to the Samaritan?

How manye myghte she have in mariage?

Yet herde I nevere tellen in myn age

25   Upon this nombre diffinicioun.

Men may devyne, and glosen up and doun,

But wel I woot, expres, withoute lye,

God bad us for to wexe and multiplye;

That gentil text kan I wel understonde.

The Prologue of the Wife of Bath's Tale

Experience, rather than written authority,

Conflicts in this world, which makes it good enough for me,

To speak of the woe that is married life.

For, Gentlemen, since I was twelve years of age,

5   *Thanks be to God, who lives in eternity,*

I have had five husbands at the church door,

For I have been married that often -

And all were worthy men in their rank.

But someone told me not long ago

10   *That since Our Lord went only once*

To a wedding in the Cana of Galilee,

That by the same example, He taught me,

I should have married no more than once.

Listen to what sharp words, were said on the occasion,

15   *Beside a well by Jesus, God and man,*

Spoke in reproach of the Samaritan.

'For thou hast had five husbands,' He said,

'And the man who has you now

Is not thine husband.' Thus He said with certainty,

20   *What He meant by that, I do not know,*

But I would ask now why that same fifth man

Was not husband to the Samaritan?

How many men could she have in marriage?

For I have never heard, in all my years,

25   *A clear definition of this number,*

[Although] men may guess and argue continuously.

But I know very well and can say, without lying,

God commanded us to be fruitful and multiply -

That noble text I know [and] well understand.

30   Eek wel I woot, he seyde, myn housbonde

          Sholde lete fader and mooder, and take to me;

          But of no nombre mencioun made he,

          Of bigamye, or of octogamye;

          Why sholde men speke of it vileynye?

35   Lo, heere the wise kyng, daun Salomon;

          I trowe he hadde wyves mo than oon-

          As, wolde God, it leveful were to me

          To be refresshed half so ofte as he!

          Which yifte of God hadde he, for alle hise wyvys!

40   No man hath swich that in this world alyve is.

          God woot, this noble kyng, as to my wit,

          The firste nyght had many a myrie fit

          With ech of hem, so wel was hym on lyve!

          Yblessed be God, that I have wedded fyve;

45   (Of whiche I have pyked out the beste,

          Bothe of here nether purs and of here cheste.

          Diverse scoles maken parfyt clerkes,

          And diverse practyk in many sondry werkes

          Maketh the werkman parfyt sekirly;

50   Of fyve husbondes scoleiyng am I.)

          Welcome the sixte, whan that evere he shal.

          For sothe I wol nat kepe me chaast in al.

          Whan myn housbonde is fro the world ygon,

          Som Cristen man shal wedde me anon.

55   For thanne th'apostle seith that I am free,

          To wedde, a Goddes half, where it liketh me.

          He seith, that to be wedded is no synne,

          Bet is to be wedded than to brynne.

          What rekketh me, thogh folk seye vileynye

60   Of shrewed Lameth and of bigamye?

30   *Also I know well, He said, that my husband*

        Should leave his father and mother, and take with me,

        But He mentioned no specific number,

        Whether of bigamy or of octogamy,

        Why should men speak of it with contempt?

35   *Lo, listen to the wise old king, lord Solomon,*

        I understand he had more than one wife -

        Would that God made it permissible for me

        To be comforted [just] half as often as he!

        What a gift from God he had for all those wives!

40   *No living man in this world has such as that.*

        God knows, this noble king, it strikes my mind,

        The first night he had many a merry adventure

        With each of them, so fortunate he was in life!

        Praise be to God, that I have wedded five!

45   *(Of whom I picked out the best*

        Both for their testicles and for their valuables

        Different schools make perfect scholars,

        And learning different methods in various works

        Certainly makes the good workman perfect,

50   *For I have been schooled by five husbands.)*

        A sixth husband is welcomed, whenever he shall arrive.

        For truth, I will not keep myself chaste for ever

        When my husband is gone from this world,

        Some Christian man shall marry me straight away

55   *For then, St Paul says that I am free*

        To wed, in God's name, where it pleases me.

        He says that to be wedded is no sin

        Better to marry than to burn.

        What care do I have, if folk speak evil

60   *Of accursed Lamech and his bigamy?*

I woot wel Abraham was an hooly man,

And Jacob eek, as ferforth as I kan,

And ech of hem hadde wyves mo than two,

And many another holy man also.

65   Whanne saugh ye evere in any manere age,

That hye God defended mariage

By expres word? I pray you, telleth me,

Or where comanded he virginitee?

I woot as wel as ye it is no drede,

70   Th'apostel, whan he speketh of maydenhede;

He seyde that precept therof hadde he noon.

Men may conseille a womman to been oon,

But conseillyng is no comandement;

He putte it in oure owene juggement.

75   For hadde God comanded maydenhede,

Thanne hadde he dampned weddyng with the dede;

And certein, if ther were no seed ysowe,

Virginitee, wherof thanne sholde it growe?

Poul dorste nat comanden, atte leeste,

80   A thyng of which his maister yaf noon heeste.

The dart is set up of virginitee;

Cacche who so may, who renneth best lat see.

But this word is nat taken of every wight,

But ther as God lust gyve it of his myght.

85   I woot wel, th'apostel was a mayde;

But nathelees, thogh that he wroot and sayde

He wolde that every wight were swich as he,

Al nys but conseil to virginitee;

And for to been a wyf, he yaf me leve

90   Of indulgence, so it is no repreve

To wedde me, if that my make dye,

I know well Abraham was holy man,

And Jacob also, as far as I know,

And each of them had more than two wives -

And many other holy men as well.

65   *When can you say, in any past era,*

That almighty God forbade marriage

By [His] express word? I pray you, tell me.

Or where He commanded virginity?

There is no doubt that I know as well as you,

70   *That when St Paul speaks about maidenhood,*

He said, he had no such commandment from the Lord.

Men may advise a woman to be one [a virgin],

But advice is not a commandment.

He left the matter to our own judgment.

75   *For had Lord God commanded maidenhood,*

He would then have damned marriage by the same deed.

And certainly, if there were no [new] seeds sown,

Where then would virgins be grown?

St Paul dared not to command us, at the least,

80   *A thing which his Master had not commanded.*

Virginity is set up to be the prize -

Catch it whosoever can; let us see who chases the best.

But this request is not meant for every person,

But [only] where God, in his power, desires it.

85   *I know well that St Paul was a virgin*

But, nevertheless, although he wrote and said

He wished that every person were such as he,

Although that is nothing but advice to be a virgin,

And so to be a wife, he gave me leave

90   *By His indulgence, so there is no disgrace*

To marry me, if my mate should die,

Withouten excepcioun of bigamye.

Al were it good no womman for to touche,

He mente, as in his bed or in his couche;

95   For peril is bothe fyr and tow t'assemble;

Ye knowe what this ensample may resemble.

This is al and som, he heeld virginitee

Moore parfit than weddyng in freletee.

Freletee clepe I, but if that he and she

100   Wolde leden al hir lyf in chastitee.

I graunte it wel, I have noon envie,

Thogh maydenhede preferre bigamye;

Hem liketh to be clene, body and goost.

Of myn estaat I nyl nat make no boost,

105   For wel ye knowe, a lord in his houshold,

He nath nat every vessel al of gold;

Somme been of tree, and doon hir lord servyse.

God clepeth folk to hym in sondry wyse,

And everich hath of God a propre yifte -

110   Som this, som that, as hym liketh shifte.

Virginitee is greet perfeccioun,

And continence eek with devocioun.

But Crist, that of perfeccioun is welle,

Bad nat every wight he sholde go selle

115   Al that he hadde, and gyve it to the poore,

And in swich wise folwe hym and his foore.

He spak to hem that wolde lyve parfitly,

And lordynges, by youre leve, that am nat I.

I wol bistowe the flour of myn age

120   In the actes and in fruyt of mariage.

Telle me also, to what conclusion

Were membres maad of generacion,

Without being accused of bigamy.

Although it is best that a woman is not touched [by a man],

He meant, in his own bed or on his couch,

95 *For there is danger when mixing both fire and tinder -*

You know what this example means.

This is the sum total: he held that virginity

Is more perfect than marrying in moral weakness.

I call it moral weakness unless he and she

100 *Would live their whole lives in chastity.*

I fully accept this, [but] I do not envy it.

Though maidenhood is preferred to bigamy.

Let those who desire being clean of body and soul,

I will not make any boast about my situation.

105 *For well you know, a lord in his household,*

He does not have every vessel [made] all of gold

Some made of wood, are [still] used in the lord's service.

God calls folk unto Him in sundry ways,

And everyone has an appropriate gift from God -

110 *Some this, some that, as it pleases Him to bestow.*

Virginity is a great perfection,

And also devout abstinence.

But Christ, who is the source of perfection,

Did not bid every person that he should go sell

115 *All that he had and give it to the poor,*

And in such manner follow Him in his foot steps.

He spoke to those that wanted to live perfectly

And gentlemen, by your leave, that is not me.

I will devote the best years of my life

120 *To the acts and fruits of marriage.*

Tell me also, for what [other] purpose

Were genitals made for reproduction,

And of so parfit wys a wright ywroght?
Trusteth right wel, they were maad for noght.
125 Close whoso wole, and seye bothe up and doun,
That they were maked for purgacioun
Of uryne, and oure bothe thynges smale
Were eek to knowe a femele from a male,
And for noon other cause, -say ye no?
130 The experience woot wel it is noght so.
So that the clerkes be nat with me wrothe,
I sey this: that they maked ben for bothe,
That is to seye, for office and for ese
Of engendrure, ther we nat God displese.
135 Why sholde men elles in hir bookes sette
That man shal yelde to his wyf hire dette?
Now wherwith sholde he make his paiement,
If he ne used his sely instrument?
Thanne were they maad upon a creature
140 To purge uryne, and eek for engendrure.
But I seye noght that every wight is holde,
That hath swich harneys as I to yow tolde,
To goon and usen hem in engendrure.
Thanne sholde men take of chastitee no cure.
145 Crist was a mayde, and shapen as a man,
And many a seint, sith that the world bigan;
Yet lyved that evere in parfit chastitee.
I nyl envye no virginitee.
Lat hem be breed of pured whete-seed,
150 And lat us wyves hoten barly-breed;
And yet with barly-breed, Mark telle kan,
Oure Lord Jhesu refresshed many a man.
In swich estaat as God hath cleped us

By such a perfect and wise craftsman?

Believe me, they were not made for nothing.

125 *Whoever interprets that way must argue continuously,*

That they were made for the passing out

Of urine, and that both of our little things

Were also to tell a female from a male,

And for no other purpose - say you not?

130 *Experience knows very well that it is not so.*

And, so the scholars will not be angry with me,

I say that they have been made for both [purposes],

That is to say, for function and for the benefit

Of reproduction, when we do not offend God.

135 *Why else should men set in their account book*

That man shall pay unto his wife her debt?

Now, with what should he make his payment,

If he did not use his blessed tool?

Then were these things were fashioned on the body

140 *For urination and also for procreation.*

But I do not say that every person is bound,

Who has such tackle, about which I told you,

To go and use it for procreation

Then men would have no care about chastity.

145 *Christ was a virgin, and shaped like a man,*

And many a saint, since this world began,

Has lived in perfect chastity.

I do not resent their virginity;

Let them be bread of purest [white] wheat-seed,

150 *And let us wives be called barley bread -*

And yet with barley bread, [as] Mark can tell [us],

Jesus Our Lord nourished many a man.

Into such status as God has called us

I wol persevere; I nam nat precius.

155 In wyfhod I wol use myn instrument

As frely as my Makere hath it sent.

If I be daungerous, God yeve me sorwe!

Myn housbonde shal it have bothe eve and morwe,

Whan that hym list come forth and paye his dette.

160 An housbonde I wol have, I wol nat lette,

Which shal be bothe my dettour and my thral,

And have his tribulacioun withal

Upon his flessh whil that I am his wyf.

I have the power durynge al my lyf

165 Upon his propre body, and noght he.

Right thus the Apostel tolde it unto me,

And bad oure housbondes for to love us weel.

Al this sentence me liketh every deel" -

Up stirte the Pardoner, and that anon;

170 "Now, dame," quod he, "by God and by Seint John!

Ye been a noble prechour in this cas.

I was aboute to wedde a wyf; allas!

What sholde I bye it on my flessh so deere?

Yet hadde I levere wedde no wyf to-yeere!"

175 "Abyde," quod she, "my tale in nat bigonne.

Nay, thou shalt drynken of another tonne,

Er that I go, shal savoure wors than ale.

And whan that I have toold thee forth my tale

Of tribulacioun in mariage,

180 Of which I am expert in al myn age,

This to seyn, myself have been the whippe, -

Than maystow chese wheither thou wolt sippe

Of thilke tonne that I shal abroche,

Be war of it, er thou to ny approche;

11

I will persevere, I am not fastidious.

155   *In wifehood I will use my womanly parts*

    As freely as my Maker sent it to me

    If I am reluctant [to provide sex], God will give me sorrow!

    My husband shall have it both evening and morning,

    Whenever he desires to come forth and pay his debt.

160   *I will not stop, I will get a husband*

    Who shall be both my debtor and my slave

    And, in addition, shall have his troubles [placed]

    Upon his body, for so long as I am his wife.

    I have the power during all my life

165   *Over his own body, not he.*

    For thus, St Paul told it to me,

    And commanded our husbands to love us dearly.

    Every part of this lesson pleases me.'

    Immediately the Pardoner jumped up.

170   *'Now lady,' he said, 'by God and by Saint John,*

    You have been a noble preacher in this matter!

    Alas, I was about to wed a wife!

    [But] why should I pay such a high price with my body?

    I would rather not wed a wife this year.'

175   *'But wait,' she said, 'my tale is not [yet] begun;*

    No, you shall drink from another barrel

    Before I go, and which shall taste worse than ale.

    And when I have told you my tale

    Of the troubles in marriage,

180   *About which, given my age, I am now an expert,*

    This to say, I have myself been the whip,

    Then may you choose whether you will sip

    Out of that very barrel which I shall tap.

    [But] beware of it, before you approach too near -

185 For I shal telle ensamples mo than ten.

   Whoso that nyl be war by othere men,

   By hym shul othere men corrected be.

   The same wordes writeth Ptholomee;

   Rede it in his Almageste, and take it there."

190 "Dame, I wolde praye yow, if youre wyl it were,"

   Seyde this Pardoner, "as ye bigan,

   Telle forth youre tale, spareth for no man,

   And teche us yonge men of your praktike."

   "Gladly," quod she, "sith it may yow like.

195 But yet I praye to al this compaignye,

   If that I speke after my fantasye,

   As taketh not agrief of that I seye,

   For myn entente nis but for to pleye."

   Now, sire, now wol I telle forth my tale,

200 As evere moote I drynken wyn or ale,

   I shal seye sooth, tho housbondes that I hadde,

   As thre of hem were goode, and two were badde.

   The thre men were goode, and riche, and olde;

   Unnethe myghte they the statut holde

205 In which that they were bounden unto me-

   Ye woot wel what I meene of this, pardee!

   As help me God, I laughe whan I thynke

   How pitously a-nyght I made hem swynke.

   And, by my fey, I tolde of it no stoor,

210 They had me yeven hir gold and hir tresoor;

   Me neded nat do lenger diligence

   To wynne hir love, or doon hem reverence,

   They loved me so wel, by God above,

   That I ne tolde no deyntee of hir love.

215 A wys womman wol sette hire evere in oon

185   *For I shall give more than ten examples.*

       Whosoever is not warned by the experience of others,

       Shall become an example by which other men are corrected.

       The same words were written by Ptolemy,

       Read it in his Almagest and find it there.'

190   *'Madam, I pray you, if you were to so will it,'*

       Said the Pardoner, 'as you began,

       Tell forth your tale, spare nothing for any man,

       And teach us younger men about your technique.'

       'Gladly,' she said, 'since it may please you.

195   *But yet I request to all this company,*

       That if I speak from my own fantasy,

       They will not take offence about the things I say,

       For my intention is for nothing but to play.

       Now, gentlemen, I will now tell you my tale.

200   *And as I may drink wine or ale continuously,*

       I shall tell the truth about the husbands that I've had,

       For three of them were good, and two were bad.

       The three good men were [both] rich and old.

       They could barely perform the contractual obligation

205   *By which they were bound to me.*

       By God, you know very well what I mean by that!

       So help me God, I laugh now when I think

       How pitifully I made them work at night

       And, by my faith, I set no store by it.

210   *They had [already] given me their gold, and their treasure;*

       [So] I no longer needed to be diligent

       To win their love, or show them respect.

       By God above, they loved me so much,

       [But] I never set [any] value on their love.

215   *A wise woman will strive continuously*

To gete hire love, ther as she hath noon.

But sith I hadde hem hoolly in myn hond,

And sith they hadde me yeven all hir lond,

What sholde I taken heede hem for to plese,

220   But it were for my profit and myn ese?

I sette hem so a-werke, by my fey,

That many a nyght they songen "weilawey!"

The bacon was nat fet for hem, I trowe,

That som men han in Essex at Dunmowe.

225   I governed hem so wel after my lawe,

That ech of hem ful blisful was, and fawe

To brynge me gaye thynges fro the fayre.

They were ful glad whan I spak to hem faire,

For, God it woot, I chidde hem spitously.

230   Now herkneth hou I baar me proprely,

Ye wise wyves, that kan understonde.

Thus shul ye speke and bere hem wrong on honde;

For half so boldely kan ther no man

Swere and lyen, as a womman kan.

235   I sey nat this by wyves that been wyse,

But if it be whan they hem mysavyse.

A wys wyf, it that she kan hir good,

Shal beren hym on hond the cow is wood,

And take witnesse of hir owene mayde,

240   Of hir assent; but herkneth how I sayde.

"Sir olde kaynard, is this thyn array?

Why is my neighebores wyf so gay?

She is honoured overal ther she gooth;

I sitte at hoom, I have no thrifty clooth.

245   What dostow at my neighebores hous?

Is she so fair? Artow so amorous?

To obtain love for herself, when she has none.

But since I had them wholly in my hand,

And since they had given me all their land,

Why should I take any heed and try to please them,

220   *Unless it was for my own profit and pleasure?*

So, by my faith, I set them so to work,

That many a night they cried out 'Alas!'

The [prize of] bacon was not brought out for them, as I believe

That some [peaceful] men have [won] in Essex at Dunmowe.

225   *I governed them so well, by my own rules,*

That each of them was happy and eager,

To bring me fine things from the market.

They were very pleased when I spoke them pleasantly;

For God knows that I scolded them relentlessly.

230   *Now hear how well I conducted myself,*

You wise wives who know and understand.

Shall you thus speak and wrongly accuse them;

For there is no man who knows how to be half as barefaced

At swearing and lying as a woman knows.

235   *I say this not to those wives who are [already] wise,*

Except when they misadvise themselves.

A wise wife, if she knows her own good,

Shall convince him that the chough is mad,

And call her own maidservant as witness

240   *In agreement; but listen to how I spoke [to him].*

Sir old Slob, is this to be your treatment [of me]?

Why is my neighbour's wife so attractively dressed?

She is honoured wherever she goes;

I sit at home, I have no suitable clothes.

245   *What do you do at my neighbour's house?*

Is she so beautiful? Are you so amorous?

What rowne ye with oure mayde? Benedicite,

Sir olde lecchour, lat thy japes be!

And if I have a gossib or a freend

250   Withouten gilt, thou chidest as a feend

If that I walke or pleye unto his hous.

Thou comest hoom as dronken as a mous

And prechest on thy bench, with yvel preef!

Thou seist to me, it is a greet meschief

255   To wedde a povre womman, for costage,

And if she be riche and of heigh parage,

Thanne seistow it is a tormentrie

To soffre hire pride and hir malencolie.

And if she be fair, thou verray knave,

260   Thou seyst that every holour wol hir have;

She may no while in chastitee abyde

That is assailled upon ech a syde.

Thou seyst, som folk desiren us for richesse,

Somme for oure shape, and somme for oure fairnesse,

265   And som for she kan outher synge or daunce,

And som for gentillesse and daliaunce,

Som for hir handes and hir armes smale;

Thus goth al to the devel by thy tale.

Thou seyst, men may nat kepe a castel wal,

270   It may so longe assailled been overal.

And if that she be foul, thou seist that she

Coveiteth every man that she may se;

For as a spaynel she wol on hym lepe

Til that she fynde som man hir to chepe;

275   Ne noon so grey goos gooth ther in the lake

As, seistow, wol been withoute make;

And seyst, it is an hard thyng for to welde

17

What do you whisper to our maidservant? Bless me!

Sir old Lecher, give up your deceit!

And if I have a confidant or a friend,

250   *Without any guilt, you will chide me like a devil*

If I walked to his house for [innocent] amusement.

You come home as drunk as a mouse,

And preach from your bench, curse you!

You say to me, it is a great misfortune,

255   *To wed a poor woman due to the expense;*

And if she's rich and of higher birth,

Then you say it's a torment

To suffer her pride and moodiness.

And if she be beautiful, you utter peasant,

260   *You say that [because] every lecher will have her.*

She will not remain chaste for long

[When] she is harassed from every side.

You say, that some men desire us for our fortunes,

Some for our figures and some for our beauty -

265   *And some, because she knows how to sing or dance,*

And some, for noble birth and sociability,

Some for her hands and for her small arms;

Thus, by your tale, [we] all go to the devil.

You say men cannot defend a castle wall

270   *That has been attacked on all sides for a lengthy time.*

And if she is unattractive, you then say that she

Lusts after every man that she sees -

Leaping on him like a spaniel

Until she finds a man who will buy her.

275   *There's not one grey goose in the lake,*

As you tell it, that would be without a mate.

You say, it is a hard thing to control

A thyng that no man wole, his thankes, helde.

Thus seistow, lorel, whan thow goost to bedde,

280   And that no wys man nedeth for to wedde,

Ne no man that entendeth unto hevene -

With wilde thonder-dynt and firy levene

Moote thy welked nekke be tobroke!

Thow seyst that droppyng houses, and eek smoke,

285   And chidyng wyves maken men to flee

Out of hir owene hous, a! benedicitee!

What eyleth swich an old man for to chide?

Thow seyst, we wyves wol oure vices hide

Til we be fast, and thanne we wol hem shewe, -

290   Wel may that be a proverbe of a shrewe!

Thou seist, that oxen, asses, hors, and houndes,

They been assayd at diverse stoundes;

Bacyns, lavours, er that men hem bye,

Spoones and stooles, and al swich housbondrye,

295   And so been pottes, clothes, and array;

But folk of wyves maken noon assay

Til they be wedded, olde dotard shrewe!

And thanne, seistow, we wol oure vices shewe.

Thou seist also, that it displeseth me

300   But if that thou wolt preyse my beautee,

And but thou poure alwey upon my face,

And clepe me "faire dame" in every place,

And but thou make a feeste on thilke day

That I was born, and make me fressh and gay,

305   And but thou do to my norice honour,

And to my chamberere withinne my bour,

And to my fadres folk and hise allyes-

Thus seistow, olde barel-ful of lyes!

19

Something that no man would willing keep

Thus, you say, scoundrel, when you go to bed,

280 *And that no wise man [thus] needs to marry,*

Nor a man who strives to enter Heaven.

[So] with furious thunder-claps and lightning

May your thin, withered neck be broken:

You say that leaking and also smoke-filled houses,

285 *And wives who scold, make men run away*

From their own house; ah, bless me!

What afflicts such an old man to make him criticise so?

You say that we wives hide our vices

Until we are married, then we show them,

290 *That may well be the proverb of a scoundrel!*

You say that oxen, asses, horses and hounds,

Have [all] been tested on various occasions

Before men will buy basins, bowls,

And spoons and stools and all such household articles,

295 *And so [too] with pots, clothes and preparation equipment -*

But men get no trial of their wives

Until they are married, old fool and scoundrel!

And then, you say, we show all our vices.

You say also that I am displeased

300 *Unless you praise and flatter my beauty,*

And constantly gaze always at my face

And call me "lovely lady" everywhere [we go],

And unless you make a feast on that day

When I was born, and give me pretty new clothes,

305 *And unless you show respect to my nurse*

As well as to my lady's maid in my bedroom,

And to my father's family and his friends -

So you say, old barrel full of lies!

And yet of oure apprentice Janekyn,
310 For his crispe heer, shynynge as gold so fyn,
And for he squiereth me bothe up and doun,
Yet hastow caught a fals suspecioun.
I wol hym noght, thogh thou were deed tomorwe!
But tel me this, why hydestow, with sorwe,
315 The keyes of my cheste awey fro me?
It is my good as wel as thyn, pardee;
What, wenestow make an ydiot of oure dame?
Now by that lord that called is Seint Jame,
Thou shalt nat bothe, thogh that thou were wood,
320 Be maister of my body and of my good;
That oon thou shalt forgo, maugree thyne eyen.
What nedeth thee of me to enquere or spyen?
I trowe thou woldest loke me in thy chiste.
Thou sholdest seye, "Wyf, go wher thee liste,
325 Taak youre disport, I wol not leve no talys,
I knowe yow for a trewe wyf, dame Alys."
We love no man that taketh kepe or charge
Wher that we goon, we wol ben at our large.
Of alle men yblessed moot he be,
330 The wise astrologien, Daun Ptholome,
That seith this proverbe in his Almageste:
`Of alle men his wysdom is the hyeste,
That rekketh nevere who hath the world in honde.'
By this proverbe thou shalt understonde,
335 Have thou ynogh, what thar thee recche or care
How myrily that othere folkes fare?
For certeyn, olde dotard, by youre leve,
Ye shul have queynte right ynogh at eve.
He is to greet a nygard, that wolde werne

And yet of our apprentice Jenkin,

310   *For his curly hair, shining like fine gold,*

And because he attends me continuously in every way,

You have been afflicted with a false suspicion:

I would give him nothing, even if you died tomorrow.

But tell me this, why do you hide, curse you,

315   *The keys to my strong-box away from me?*

By God, these are my goods as well as yours;

What, why would you make an idiot of the lady of the house?

Now by the lord who is called Saint James,

You shall not have both, even if you scold like crazy,

320   *[And] be master of both my body and my goods;*

You must forego one, despite anything you can do.

Why do you need to make enquiries of me or spy?

I think you'd like to lock me in your chest!

You should say: 'Wife, go wherever you like,

325   *Have your fun, I will not believe any [malicious] tales.*

I know you to be a good wife, lady Alison.'

We love no man that watches over us or commands

Where we go, for we will be at liberty.

Of all men the most blessed may he be,

330   *That wise astrologer, lord Ptolemy,*

Who tells this proverb in his Almagest:

"The men with the highest wisdom,

Who cares nothing about who has control in the world."

By this proverb you shall understand:

335   *[That] if you have enough, why are you concerned or care*

How merrily all other folks live?

For certain, senile fool, by your leave,

You shall have plenty of my pleasing thing tonight.

He is too great a miser if he would refuse

340   A man to lighte his candle at his lanterne;

He shal have never the lasse light, pardee,

Have thou ynogh, thee thar nat pleyne thee.

Thou seyst also, that if we make us gay

With clothyng and with precious array,

345   That it is peril of oure chastitee:

And yet, with sorwe, thou most enforce thee,

And seye thise wordes in the Apostles name,

"In habit, maad with chastitee and shame,

Ye wommen shul apparaille yow," quod he,

350   "And noght in tressed heer and gay perree,

As perles, ne with gold, ne clothes riche."

After thy text, ne after thy rubriche

I wol nat wirche, as muchel as a gnat!

Thou seydest this, that I was lyk a cat;

355   For whoso wolde senge a cattes skyn,

Thanne wolde the cat wel dwellen in his in.

And if the cattes skyn be slyk and gay,

She wol nat dwelle in house half a day,

But forth she wole, er any day be dawed,

360   To shewe hir skyn, and goon a-caterwawed.

This is to seye, if I be gay, sire shrewe,

I wol renne out, my borel for to shewe.

Sire olde fool, what eyleth thee to spyen,

Thogh thou preye Argus, with his hundred eyen,

365   To be my warde-cors, as he kan best,

In feith, he shal nat kepe me but me lest;

Yet koude I make his berd, so moot I thee.

Thou seydest eek, that ther been thynges thre,

The whiche thynges troublen al this erthe,

370   And that no wight ne may endure the ferthe.

340   *To light a man's candle from his lantern*

    By God, he will never have any less light [for himself]

    Since you have enough, there's nothing to complain about.

    You also say that if we make ourselves attractive

    With clothing, and with expensive adornments,

345   *That it endangers our chastity;*

    Indeed, bad luck to you, you strengthen your stance

    And repeat these words in St Paul's name:

    "In clothing made for chastity, not shame,

    You women shall dress yourselves," he said,

350   *"And not with plaited hair, or jewellery,*

    Like pearls, nor with gold, or expensive gowns;"

    About your text and your interpretation

    I will not follow them any more than I would a gnat.

    You said this, that I was like a cat;

355   *For whoever would singe a cat's fur,*

    Then the cat would remain inside the house;

    And if the cat's coat be all sleek and beautiful,

    She will not stay in the house even half a day,

    But she will go out, before the dawn of any day,

360   *To show her fur and caterwaul and play.*

    This is to say, Sir Scoundrel, if I'm finely dressed,

    I would run out to show my clothes.

    Sir old fool, what afflicts you to spy [on me]?

    Though you ask Argus, with his hundred eyes,

365   *To be my body-guard, as he knows best,*

    In faith, he shall not watch me, unless I am willing;

    Yet, I could deceive him - trust me!

    You also say, that there are three things -

    Which are a trouble on this earth,

370   *And that no person could endure the fourth.*

O leeve sire shrewe, Jesu shorte thy lyf!

Yet prechestow, and seyst an hateful wyf

Yrekened is for oon of thise meschances.

Been ther none othere maner resemblances

375 That ye may likne youre parables to,

But if a sely wyf be oon of tho?

Thou likenest wommenes love to helle,

To bareyne lond, ther water may nat dwelle.

Thou liknest it also to wilde fyr;

380 The moore it brenneth, the moore it hath desir

To consume every thyng that brent wole be.

Thou seyest, right as wormes shende a tree,

Right so a wyf destroyeth hir housbond.

This knowe they, that been to wyves bonde."

385 Lordynges, right thus, as ye have understonde,

Baar I stifly myne olde housbondes on honde,

That thus they seyden in hir dronkenesse;

And al was fals, but that I took witnesse

On Janekyn and on my nece also.

390 O lord! The pyne I dide hem, and the wo

Ful giltelees, by Goddes sweete pyne!

For as an hors I koude byte and whyne,

I koude pleyne, thogh I were in the gilt,

Or elles often tyme hadde I been spilt.

395 Who so that first to mille comth first grynt;

I pleyned first, so was oure werre ystynt.

They were ful glad to excuse hem ful blyve

Of thyng of which they nevere agilte hir lyve.

Of wenches wolde I beren hym on honde,

400 Whan that for syk unnethes myghte he stonde,

Yet tikled it his herte, for that he!

O dear Sir Rogue, may Christ cut short your life!

Yet you preach and say that a hateful wife

Is reckoned to be one of those misfortunes.

[But] are there no other kinds of comparisons

375 *That you could use as an analogy in your parables,*

Unless [using] an innocent wife is one of them?

You liken women's love to Hell,

To desert land where water does not collect.

You also liken it to [inextinguishable] Greek fire -

380 *The more it burns, the more it craves*

To consume everything that can be burned.

You say that just as worms destroy a tree,

Does a wife subject her husband to hardship?

Men who that are bound to their wives know this

385 *Gentlemen, as you have understood, in this very way,*

I resolutely swore that my old husbands

Had said these things in their drunkenness;

[But] all of this was a lie, but I brought the witness

Of Jenkin and of my dear niece also.

390 *O Lord, the pain and the misery I caused them,*

[Yet] by God's suffering, they were innocent!

For like a stallion I could bite and neigh.

Although the guilt was all mine, I could complain,

If not, there were many times when I would have been done for.

395 *For whoever come to the mill first, grinds first*

I complained first, so our war was ended.

They were very happy to excuse themselves very quickly

For something they had never done in their lives.

I would accuse him of [going] with young girls,

400 *When, due to sickness, he could hardly stand.*

Yet it tickled his heart, since he thereby

Wende that I hadde of hym so greet chiertee.

I swoor that al my walkynge out by nyghte

Was for t'espye wenches that he dighte.

405   Under that colour hadde I many a myrthe;

For al swich wit is yeven us in oure byrthe,

Deceite, wepyng, spynnyng, God hath yive

To wommen kyndely whil they may lyve.

And thus of o thyng I avaunte me,

410   Atte ende I hadde the bettre in ech degree,

By sleighte, or force, or by som maner thyng,

As by continueel murmur or grucchyng.

Namely a bedde hadden they meschaunce;

Ther wolde I chide and do hem no plesaunce,

415   I wolde no lenger in the bed abyde,

If that I felte his arm over my syde

Til he had maad his raunsoun unto me;

Thanne wolde I suffre hym do his nycetee.

And therfore every man this tale I telle,

420   Wynne who so may, for al is for to selle;

With empty hand men may none haukes lure.

For wynnyng wolde I al his lust endure

And make me a feyned appetit;

And yet in bacon hadde I nevere delit;

425   That made me that evere I wolde hem chide.

For thogh the pope hadde seten hem biside,

I wolde nat spare hem at hir owene bord,

For by my trouthe I quitte hem word for word.

As help me verray God omnipotent,

430   Though I right now sholde make my testament,

I ne owe hem nat a word, that it nys quit.

I broghte it so aboute by my wit,

27

Believed that I had great love for him.

I swore that my wandering about at night

Was to spy on girls with whom he was having sex

405   *Under that pretence I had a lot of fun*

For all such skills are given to us at birth.

Deceit, weeping, spinning skills, God has given

To women, naturally, for their whole lives.

And thus of one thing I can boast,

410   *In the end, I got the best of each of them,*

By trick, or force, or by some such device,

Such as by constant complaints or grumbling -

Especially if they suffered a misfortune in bed,

I would then scold them and give them no pleasure;

415   *I would not stay in the bed any longer*

If I felt his arm across my side,

Until he had paid his ransom to me;

Then would I let him satisfy his lust.

And, therefore, to all men I will tell this tale,

420   *Everyone can win, for everything is up for sale.*

Men cannot lure a hawk with an empty hand -

To make profit, I would endure his lust.

And pretend to have a sexual desire.

Yet I have never taken pleasure from old meat,

425   *And that is why I used to scold so much.*

For even if the pope was sitting beside them

I would not have spared them, even at their own table,

For by my truth, I paid them back, word for word.

So help me, the true omnipotent God,

430   *If I was to make my will right away,*

I would owe them not one word that has not been repaid.

So, by my cunning, I brought it about,

That they moste yeve it up as for the beste,

Or elles hadde we nevere been in reste.

435 For thogh he looked as a wood leon,

Yet sholde he faille of his conclusioun.

Thanne wolde I seye, "Goode lief, taak keep,

How mekely looketh Wilkyn oure sheep!

Com neer, my spouse, lat me ba thy cheke!

440 Ye sholde been al pacient and meke,

And han a sweete spiced conscience,

Sith ye so preche of Jobes pacience.

Suffreth alwey, syn ye so wel kan preche,

And but ye do, certein we shal yow teche

445 That it is fair to have a wyf in pees.

Oon of us two moste bowen, doutelees;

And sith a man is moore resonable,

Than womman is, ye moste been suffrable."

What eyleth yow to grucche thus and grone?

450 Is it for ye wolde have my queynte allone?

Wy, taak it al! lo, have it every deel!

Peter! I shrewe yow, but ye love it weel;

For if I wolde selle my bele chose,

I koude walke as fressh as is a rose

455 But I wol kepe it for youre owene tooth.

Ye be to blame, by God! I sey yow sooth."

Swiche manere wordes hadde we on honde.

Now wol I speken of my fourthe housbonde.

My fourthe housbonde was a revelour -

460 This is to seyn, he hadde a paramour -

And I was yong and ful of ragerye,

Stibourn and strong, and joly as a pye.

Wel koude I daunce to an harpe smale,

29

That they were forced to give up, as their best choice,

Or otherwise we would never have had rest.

435   *For although he looked like a mad lion,*

He would still fail to achieve his wishes.

Then would I say: 'My dear, take heed

Of how meek Willie, our old sheep, looks.

Come near, my spouse, let me kiss your cheek!

440   *You should always be patient and meek,*

And have a pleasing disposition,

Since you preach so about Job's patience,

Suffer always, since you know how to preach so well,

And, unless you do, [you can] be sure that we'll teach

445   *That it is desirable to have a peaceful wife.*

Certainly, one of us two must yield,

And since a man is more reasonable,

Than is a woman, you are most able to endure hardship.

What afflicts you that you grumble and groan in such a way?

450   *Is it because you want my vagina all to yourself?*

Okay take it all. Look, have every bit of it.

By St Peter! I would curse you if you didn't love it so much!

For if I was to sell my beautiful thing,

I could walk out as fresh as a rose,

455   *But I will keep it all for you.*

You are to blame, by God! I tell the truth

Such were the manner of words we had [between us].

'Now will I tell you about my fourth husband.

My fourth husband was a reveller,

460   *That is to say, he kept a mistress;*

Then, I was young and full of passion,

Stubborn and strong and as chatty as a magpie.

I could dance very well to a small harp,

And synge, ywis, as any nyghtyngale,

465   Whan I had dronke a draughte of sweete wyn.

Metellius, the foule cherl, the swyn,

That with a staf birafte his wyf hire lyf,

For she drank wyn, thogh I hadde been his wyf,

He sholde nat han daunted me fro drynke.

470   And after wyn on Venus moste I thynke,

For al so siker as cold engendreth hayl,

A likerous mouth moste han a likerous tayl.

In wommen vinolent is no defence,

This knowen lecchours by experience.

475   But, Lord Crist! whan that it remembreth me

Upon my yowthe and on my jolitee,

It tikleth me aboute myn herte roote.

Unto this day it dooth myn herte boote

That I have had my world, as in my tyme.

480   But age, allas, that al wole envenyme,

Hath me biraft my beautee and my pith!

Lat go, farewel, the devel go therwith!

The flour is goon, ther is namoore to telle,

The bren as I best kan, now moste I selle;

485   But yet to be right myrie wol I fonde.

Now wol I tellen of my fourthe housbonde.

I seye, I hadde in herte greet despit

That he of any oother had delit;

But he was quit, by God and by Seint Joce!

490   I made hym of the same wode a croce;

Nat of my body in no foul manere,

But certeinly, I made folk swich cheere

That in his owene grece I made hym frye

For angre and for verray jalousye.

And sing as well as any nightingale,

465   *When I had drunk a draught of sweet wine.*

Metellius, the foul peasant. the swine,

Killed his wife with a staff,

Because she had drunk wine, although If I had been his wife,

He would never have frightened me away from drink.

470   *For after wine, I always think of Venus,*

For just as surely as cold produces hail,

A gluttonous mouth must have a lecherous tail

In women, drunkenness is not a defence,

This all lechers know by experience.

475   *But Lord Christ! When I remember*

My youth and my gaiety,

It tickles me to the bottom of my heart

Right up to today, my heart sings in salute

That, in my lifetime, I have had the world.

480   *But age which, alas, poisons everything,*

Has taken away my beauty and my vigour.

Let it go! Farewell! And may the devil go with it!

The flour is gone, there is no more to tell,

I must now hawk around the rough bran as best as I know how;

485   *But I will try to be very merry and*

Will now tell you about my fourth husband.

I say that I had great anger in my heart

When he enjoyed himself with another woman.

But God and by Saint Judocus paid him back!

490   *I made him a cross of that same wood [he had used against me] -*

But not with my body in a disgusting way,

But truly, I was so cheery with other folk

That I made him fry in his own grease

For [my] anger and for true jealousy.

495   By God, in erthe I was his purgatorie,

For which I hope his soule be in glorie,

For, God it woot, he sat ful ofte and song

Whan that his shoo ful bitterly hym wrong!

Ther was no wight save God and he, that wiste

500   In many wise how soore I hym twiste.

He deyde whan I cam fro Jerusalem,

And lith ygrave under the roode-beem,

Al is his tombe noght so curyus

As was the sepulcre of hym Daryus,

505   Which that Appelles wroghte subtilly.

It nys but wast to burye hym preciously,

Lat hym fare-wel, God yeve his soule reste,

He is now in his grave, and in his cheste.

Now of my fifthe housbonde wol I telle.

510   God lete his soule nevere come in helle!

And yet was he to me the mooste shrewe;

That feele I on my ribbes al by rewe,

And evere shal, unto myn endyng day.

But in oure bed he was ful fressh and gay,

515   And therwithal so wel koude he me glose

Whan that he solde han my bele chose,

That thogh he hadde me bet on every bon

He koude wynne agayn my love anon.

I trowe I loved hym beste, for that he

520   Was of his love daungerous to me.

We wommen han, if that I shal nat lye,

In this matere a queynte fantasye;

Wayte what thyng we may nat lightly have,

Therafter wol we crie al day and crave.

525   Forbede us thyng, and that desiren we;

495   *By God, I was his purgatory on Earth,*

         For which I hope his soul now lives in glory,

         For God knows, many a time he sat and cried out

         When his shoe pinched him badly.

         There was no person, save God and he, who knew

500   *How, in so many ways, I would torture him.*

         He died when I returned from Jerusalem,

         And lies entombed before the great chancel screen,

         Although his tomb is not so lavish

         As was Darius' grave,

505   *Which Apelles built so skilfully,*

         It was nothing but waste to bury him expensively.

         Let him fare well. God give his soul good rest,

         He is now in his grave, in his coffin.

         I will now tell you about my fifth husband.

510   *May God ensure his soul never goes to Hell!*

         And yet he was also the most brutal to me.

         I can still feel the pain in each rib, one after the other,

         And shall always do so, until my dying day.

         But in our bed he was very lively and jovial,

515   *And, furthermore, he knew very well how to talk me round,*

         Whenever he wanted my beautiful thing,

         That although he had beaten every bone of my body,

         He could re-win my love very quickly.

         I believe I loved him best of all, for he

520   *Was very sparing when giving his love to me.*

         I shall not lie, we women have,

         A peculiar fantasy in love matters.

         We look out for whatever things we cannot easily have,

         And thereafter we will cry all day and crave for it.

525   *Forbid us something, and we will desire it more -*

Preesse on us faste, and thanne wol we fle;

With daunger oute we al oure chaffare.

Greet prees at market maketh deere ware,

And to greet cheep is holde at litel prys;

530   This knoweth every womman that is wys.

My fifthe housbonde, God his soule blesse,

Which that I took for love and no richesse,

He somtyme was a clerk of Oxenford,

And hadde left scole, and wente at hom to bord

535   With my gossib, dwellynge in oure toun,

God have hir soule! hir name was Alisoun.

She knew myn herte and eek my privetee

Bet than oure parisshe preest, as moot I thee.

To hir biwreyed I my conseil al,

540   For hadde myn housbonde pissed on a wal,

Or doon a thyng that sholde han cost his lyf,

To hir, and to another worthy wyf,

And to my nece, which that I loved weel,

I wolde han toold his conseil every deel.

545   And so I dide ful often, God it woot,

That made his face ful often reed and hoot

For verray shame, and blamed hym-self, for he

Had toold to me so greet a pryvetee.

And so bifel that ones, in a Lente -

550   So often tymes I to my gossyb wente,

For evere yet I loved to be gay,

And for to walke in March, Averill, and May,

Fro hous to hous to heere sondry talys -

That Jankyn Clerk and my gossyb, dame Alys,

555   And I myself into the feeldes wente.

Myn housbonde was at London al that Lente;

[But] force a thing on us and then we will run away.

Women lay out our desirable wares only reluctantly,

{For] great crowds at the market make goods dearer,

And what is too abundant commands a low price;

530   *Every wise woman knows this.*

My fifth husband, may God bless his spirit!

Whom I took for love, and not riches,

Had been sometime a student at Oxford,

And had left college and came home to lodge

535   *With my best friend, who lived in our town,*

God save her soul! Her name was Alison.

She knew my heart and all my secrets

Better than our parish priest, I must say.

I confided all my secrets to her.

540   *For if my husband had pissed against a wall,*

Or had done a thing that could have cost him his life,

To her and to another worthy wife,

And to my niece whom I have always loved,

I would have told his secrets in every detail,

545   *And, God knows, I did so many times,*

Which often made his face become very red and hot

Out of true shame, and blamed himself that he

Had told me such a great secret.

So, it happened one day in Lent

550   *For I often went to visit my closest friend,*

Since I always loved to be happy and jolly

And during March, April, and May, to go walking

From house to house, to hear the latest gossip

That Jenkin the secretary, and my best friend lady Alice,

555   *And myself went into the meadows.*

My husband was in London for all of that Lent

I hadde the bettre leyser for to pleye,

And for to se, and eek for to be seye

Of lusty folk; what wiste I, wher my grace

560   Was shapen for to be, or in what place?

Therfore I made my visitaciouns

To vigilies and to processiouns,

To prechyng eek, and to thise pilgrimages,

To pleyes of myracles, and to mariages;

565   And wered upon my gaye scarlet gytes.

Thise wormes ne thise motthes, ne thise mytes,

Upon my peril, frete hem never a deel;

And wostow why? for they were used weel!

Now wol I tellen forth what happed me.

570   I seye, that in the feeldes walked we,

Til trewely we hadde swich daliance,

This clerk and I, that of my purveiance

I spak to hym, and seyde hym, how that he,

If I were wydwe, sholde wedde me.

575   For certeinly, I sey for no bobance,

Yet was I nevere withouten purveiance

Of mariage, n'of othere thynges eek.

I holde a mouses herte nat worth a leek

That hath but oon hole for to sterte to,

580   And if that faille, thanne is al ydo.

I bar hym on honde, he hadde enchanted me, -

My dame taughte me that soutiltee.

And eek I seyde, I mette of hym al nyght,

He wolde han slayn me as I lay upright,

585   And al my bed was ful of verray blood;

But yet I hope that he shal do me good,

For blood bitokeneth gold, as me was taught-

I had a better chance to play,

And to watch, and to be seen

By lusty folk. What did I know what my fate

560 *Was destined to be, or in what place?*

Therefore, I made my visits

To vigils and religious processions,

Listening to preachers also, and to sites of pilgrimage,

To watch miracle plays, and to marriages,

565 *And wore my pretty scarlet dresses.*

The worms nor the moths nor the mites,

Never ate into them, I swear,

And do you know why? For they were used so often!

Now will I tell you what happened to me.

570 *I say that we three walked in the meadows,*

Until, truly, we became very flirtatious,

This learned man and I, that with thoughts of my future provision,

I spoke to him and told him that he,

If I was to become a widow, should marry me.

575 *For certainly, I do not mean to boast,*

But I was never without propositions

Of marriage, nor of other things as well.

I hold a mouse's life is worth nothing

[If] he has only one hole into which he can run,

580 *And if that [hole] fails, then he is done.*

I falsely accused him that he had enchanted me -

My mother taught me that trick.

And I also said I'd dreamed about him all night,

He would have killed me as I lay on my back,

585 *And that my bed was full of blood;*

But yet, I hoped that he would do me good,

For I was taught that blood represents gold-

And al was fals, I dremed of it right naught,

But as I folwed ay my dames loore

590 As wel of this, as of othere thynges moore.

But now sir, lat me se, what I shal seyn?

A ha, by God, I have my tale ageyn.

Whan that my fourthe housbonde was on beere,

I weep algate, and made sory cheere,

595 As wyves mooten, for it is usage-

And with my coverchief covered my visage;

But for that I was purveyed of a make,

I wepte but smal, and that I undertake.

To chirche was myn housbonde born amorwe

600 With neighebores that for hym maden sorwe;

And Janekyn oure clerk was oon of tho.

As help me God! whan that I saugh hym go

After the beere, me thoughte he hadde a paire

Of legges and of feet so clene and faire,

605 That al myn herte I yaf unto his hoold.

He was, I trowe, a twenty wynter oold,

And I was fourty, if I shal seye sooth,

But yet I hadde alwey a coltes tooth.

Gat-tothed I was, and that bicam me weel,

610 I hadde the prente of Seinte Venus seel.

As help me God, I was a lusty oon,

And faire, and riche, and yong, and wel bigon,

And trewely, as myne housbondes tolde me,

I hadde the beste *quonyam* myghte be.

615 For certes, I am al Venerien

In feelynge, and myn herte is Marcien.

Venus me yaf my lust, my likerousnesse,

And Mars yaf me my sturdy hardynesse.

[Yet] all of this was a lie, I never dreamed about this,
But I followed my mother's teaching

590   *On this matter, as well as on many more things.*
    But now, sir, let me see, what was I going to say?
    Aha, by God, I know! I have my tale to tell.
    When my fourth husband lay dead in his coffin,
    I wept continuously, and had a sorrowful expression,

595   *As wives must always do, for it is the custom,*
    And I covered my face with a veil -
    But since I was provided with a mate,
    I can say that I wept only a little.
    My husband was carried to church the next morning

600   *By neighbours that who mourned for him -*
    And our Jenkin our secretary, was one of them.
    So help me God, when I saw him
    Follow the coffin, I thought he had a pair
    Of legs and feet so neat and attractive

605   *That I gave him all my heart to hold.*
    He was, I think, twenty winters old,
    And I was forty, if I am to tell the truth,
    But then I always had the appetite for the young.
    Gap-toothed I was, and that suited me well;

610   *I had the print of holy Venus' seal.*
    So help me God, I was a lively one,
    And fair and rich and young and well-off -
    And truly, as my husbands all told me,
    I had the best belle chose there could be.

615   *For certain, I am of Venus*
    Emotionally, whilst my character is of Mars.
    Venus gave me my lust, my wantonness,
    And Mars gave me my obstinate boldness.

Myn ascendent was Taur, and Mars therinne,

620 Allas, allas, that evere love was synne!

I folwed ay myn inclinacioun

By vertu of my constellacioun;

That made me I koude noght withdrawe

My chambre of Venus from a good felawe.

625 Yet have I Martes mark upon my face,

And also in another privee place.

For God so wys be my savacioun,

I ne loved nevere by no discrecioun,

But evere folwede myn appetit,

630 Al were he short, or long, or blak, or whit.

I took no kep, so that he liked me,

How poore he was, ne eek of what degree.

What sholde I seye, but at the monthes ende

This joly clerk Jankyn, that was so hende

635 Hath wedded me with greet solempnytee,

And to hym yaf I al the lond and fee

That evere was me yeven therbifoore;

But afterward repented me ful soore;

He nolde suffre nothyng of my list.

640 By God, he smoot me ones on the lyst

For that I rente out of his book a leef,

That of the strook myn ere wax al deef.

Stibourne I was as is a leonesse,

And of my tonge a verray jangleresse,

645 And walke I wolde, as I had doon biforn,

From hous to hous, although he had it sworn,

For which he often-tymes wolde preche,

And me of olde Romayn geestes teche,

How he Symplicius Gallus lefte his wyf,

[On my birth] Taurus was in ascendance, with Mars therein,

620 *Alas, alas, that ever love was [considered] a sin!*

I always followed my inclination

By virtue of my star sign

Which made me so that I could never refuse

My love-chamber from a good fellow.

625 *Yet have I a red mark upon my face,*

And also in another private place.

For as God, so wise, will be my salvation,

have never loved in moderation,

But have always followed my own appetite,

630 *Whether he was short or tall, or black or white,*

I took no heed, so long that he pleasured me,

How poor he was, nor even of what rank.

What should I say, save, at the month's end,

This jolly secretary Jenkin, that was so handsome

635 *Had married me with full ceremony,*

And to him I gave all the land absolutely

That had ever been given to me beforehand,

But later, I was bitterly regretful.

He never allowed me to have my wishes.

640 *By God, he struck me once on the ear,*

Because I tore a page from out of his book,

From that strike my ear became completely deaf.

I was as stubborn as a lioness,

And with my tongue like a true chatterbox,

645 *I would walk, as I had done before,*

From house to house, although he had sworn that I should not.

For which he would often preach

And lecture me about old Roman tales,

How a man called Symplicius Gallus left his wife

650   And hir forsook for terme of al his lyf,

Noght but for open-heveded he hir say,

Lookynge out at his dore, upon a day.

Another Romayn tolde he me by name,

That for his wyf was at a someres game

655   Withoute his wityng, he forsook hir eke.

And thanne wolde he upon his Bible seke

That like proverbe of Ecclesiaste,

Where he comandeth, and forbedeth faste,

Man shal nat suffre his wyf go roule aboute,

660   Thanne wolde he seye right thus, withouten doute:

"Who so that buyldeth his hous al of salwes,

And priketh his blynde hors over the falwes,

And suffreth his wyf to go seken halwes,

Is worthy to been hanged on the galwes!"

665   But al for noght, I sette noght an hawe

Of his proverbes, n'of his olde sawe,

Ne I wolde nat of hym corrected be.

I hate hym that my vices telleth me;

And so doo mo, God woot, of us than I.

670   This made hym with me wood al outrely,

I nolde noght forbere hym in no cas.

Now wol I seye yow sooth, by seint Thomas,

Why that I rente out of his book a leef,

For which he smoot me so that I was deef.

675   He hadde a book that gladly, nyght and day,

For his desport he wolde rede alway.

He cleped it Valerie and Theofraste,

At whiche book he lough alwey ful faste.

And eek ther was som tyme a clerk at Rome,

680   A cardinal that highte Seint Jerome,

650   *And abandoned her for the rest of his life*

        For nothing more than her going bare-headed, he said

        [When] looking out of his door one day.

        He told me about another Roman, by name,

        Who, because his wife was at a summer festivity

655   *Without him knowing, he also abandoned her.*

        And then he would search inside his Bible for

        That proverb of Ecclesiasticus

        Where he commanded, and strictly forbade,

        That a man should suffer his wife to go gadding about;

660   *He would then say as follows, without doubt:*

           "Whosoever that builds his house out of sallows,

           And spurs his blind horse over the fallows,

           And allows his wife to go alone seeking hallows,

           Is worthy to be hanged upon the gallows."

665   *But that was all for nothing, I had no regard*

        For his proverbs, nor for his old sayings,

        Nor yet would I be corrected by him.

        I hate someone who tells me about my shortcomings:

        God knows, and so do more of us than just myself.

670   *This made him insanely angry with me,*

        [But] in no event would I not submit to him.

        Now, by Saint Thomas, I will tell you the truth,

        About why I tore a leaf out of his book,

        For which he struck me so that I became deaf.

675   *He had a book that happily, night and day,*

        He would always read for his amusement.

        He called it 'Valerius' and 'Theophrastus',

        At which book he would always laugh most heartily.

        And also, there once was a cleric at Rome,

680   *A cardinal, that was called Saint Jerome,*

That made a book agayn Jovinian,

In whiche book eek ther was Tertulan,

Crisippus, Trotula, and Helowys,

That was abbesse nat fer fro Parys,

685 And eek the Parables of Salomon,

Ovides Art, and bookes many on,

And alle thise were bounden in o volume,

And every nyght and day was his custume

Whan he hadde leyser and vacacioun

690 From oother worldly occupacioun

To reden on this book of wikked wyves.

He knew of hem mo legendes and lyves

Than been of goode wyves in the Bible.

For trusteth wel, it is an impossible

695 That any clerk wol speke good of wyves,

But if it be of hooly seintes lyves,

Ne of noon oother womman never the mo.

Who peyntede the leon, tel me, who?

By God! if wommen hadde writen stories,

700 As clerkes han withinne hire oratories,

They wolde han writen of men moore wikkednesse

Than all the mark of Adam may redresse.

The children of Mercurie and Venus

Been in hir wirkyng ful contrarius,

705 Mercurie loveth wysdam and science,

And Venus loveth ryot and dispence.

And for hire diverse disposicioun

Ech falleth in otheres exaltacioun,

And thus, God woot, Mercurie is desolat

710 In Pisces, wher Venus is exaltat;

And Venus falleth ther Mercurie is reysed.

Who made a book against Jovinian,

In which book, too, there was also Tertullian,

Chrysippus, Trotula, and Heloise -

Who was an abbess not far from Paris -

685   *And also the Proverbs of King Solomon,*

Ovid's Art, and many other books.

And all these were bound in one volume.

And every night and day it was his custom,

When he had leisure and free time

690   *From all his other worldly occupation,*

To read, this book about wicked wives.

He knew more of those legends and lives

Than of all the good wives contained in the Bible.

For trust me, it is an impossibility,

695   *That any cleric will speak well of wives,*

Unless it is about the holy saints' lives,

But never of any other women.

Who first painted the lion? Tell me, who?

By God, if women had written stories,

700   *As the scholars have within their study rooms,*

They would have written more about men's wickedness

Than all the male gender could redress.

The children of Mercury [scholars] and Venus [lovers]

Are directly opposite in their actions,

705   *For Mercury loves wisdom and knowledge,*

And Venus loves revelry and extravagance.

And [because] of their different natures,

Each falls when the other is in ascendance.

And thus, God knows, Mercury is helpless and powerless

710   *In Pisces, where Venus is exalted -*

And Venus falls when Mercury rises.

Therfore no womman of no clerk is preysed.

The clerk, whan he is oold and may noght do

Of Venus werkes worth his olde sho,

715 Thanne sit he doun, and writ in his dotage

That wommen kan nat kepe hir mariage.

But now to purpos, why I tolde thee

That I was beten for a book, pardee.

Upon a nyght Jankyn, that was oure sire,

720 Redde on his book as he sat by the fire

Of Eva first, that for hir wikkednesse

Was al mankynde broght to wrecchednesse,

For which that Jhesu Crist hymself was slayn,

That boghte us with his herte blood agayn.

725 Lo, heere expres of womman may ye fynde,

That womman was the los of al mankynde.

Tho redde he me how Sampson loste hise heres,

Slepynge, his lemman kitte it with hir sheres,

Thurgh whiche tresoun loste he bothe hise yen.

730 Tho redde he me, if that I shal nat lyen,

Of Hercules and of his Dianyre,

That caused hym to sette hymself afyre.

No thyng forgat he the penaunce and wo

That Socrates hadde with hise wyves two,

735 How Xantippa caste pisse upon his heed.

This sely man sat stille as he were deed;

He wiped his heed, namoore dorste he seyn

But, "Er that thonder stynte, comth a reyn."

Of Phasipha, that was the queene of Crete,

740 For shrewednesse hym thoughte the tale swete-

Fy! Speke namoore - it is a grisly thyng -

Of hir horrible lust and hir likyng.

Therefore, no woman is praised by a cleric.

[Yet] the cleric, when he is old and cannot do [any]

Of Venus' work worth his worn-out shoe,

715   Then, he sits down and writes in his old age

That women do not know how to keep their marriage vows.

But now [back] to the point, why I told you

That, by God, I was beaten for a book.

One night, Jenkin, the master of our household,

720   Read in his book, as he sat by the fire

About the Eve who, by her wickedness, first

Brought all mankind to wretchedness,

For which Lord Jesus Christ Himself was slain,

That again redeemed us with His heart's blood.

725   Lo here, you can find it expressly said of woman,

That woman was the ruin of all mankind.

Then he read to me about how Samson lost his hair,

[While] sleeping, his lover cut it with her shears.

By reason of this treason he lost both of his eyes.

730   Then he read to me, no word of a lie,

Of Hercules, and his [wife] Deianira

Who caused him to set himself on fire.

Nor did he forget the suffering and woe

That Socrates had with his two wives -

735   How Xantippe threw urine over his head -

This hapless man sat still, as if he were dead,

He wiped his head, daring to say no more

Except 'before the thunder ceases, comes the rain.'

Of Pasiphae, who was the queen of Crete [who copulated with a bull],

740   For depravity, he thought the story was pleasing-

Fie! Speak no more- it is a disgusting thing -

About her horrible lust and her sexual desires.

Of Clitermystra for hire lecherye,

That falsly made hir housbonde for to dye,

745   He redde it with ful good devocioun.

He tolde me eek for what occasioun

Amphiorax at Thebes loste his lyf.

Myn housbonde hadde a legende of his wyf

Eriphilem, that for an ouche of gold

750   Hath prively unto the Grekes told

Wher that hir housbonde hidde hym in a place,

For which he hadde at Thebes sory grace.

Of Lyvia tolde he me, and of Lucye,

They bothe made hir housbondes for to dye,

755   That oon for love, that oother was for hate.

Lyvia hir housbonde, on an even late,

Empoysoned hath, for that she was his fo.

Lucia, likerous, loved hir housbonde so,

That for he sholde alwey upon hire thynke,

760   She yaf hym swich a manere love-drynke

That he was deed, er it were by the morwe.

And thus algates housbondes han sorw.

Thanne tolde he me, how that Latumyus

Compleyned unto his felawe Arrius,

765   That in his gardyn growed swich a tree,

On which he seyde how that hise wyves thre

Hanged hemself, for herte despitus.

"O leeve brother," quod this Arrius,

"Yif me a plante of thilke blissed tree,

770   And in my gardyn planted it shal bee."

Of latter date of wyves hath he red,

That somme han slayn hir housbondes in hir bed,

And lete hir lecchour dighte hir al the nyght,

49

Of Clytemnystra, for her lechery,

That wrongly caused her husband's death,

745   *He read it with great interest,.*

He also told me the cause why

Amphiaraus lost his life at Thebes;

My husband had a story about his wife

Eriphyle, who, for a gold brooch,

750   *Secretly told the Greeks*

Where her husband had his hiding place,

For which he met a sorry fate at Thebes.

Of Livia and Lucie he told me,

Both caused their husbands to die,

755   *One for love, the other for hate.*

Late one evening, For her husband, Livia

Made him a poisoned drink, for she was his enemy.

Lucia, so amorous, had such love for her husband

So that he would always think about her

760   *She gave him such a form of love-potion,*

That he was dead before the morning.

And thus, in either case, husbands came to sorrow.

Then did he tell how one Latumius

Complained to his friend Arrius,

765   *That in his garden there grew such a tree*

On which, he said, his three wives,

Had hanged themselves with a spiteful heart.

'O dear brother,' this Arrius said,

Give me a graft from that same blessed tree

770   *And it shall be planted in my garden!'*

He read about wives in later times,

That some had killed their husbands in their bed,

And let their lovers have sex with them all night

Whan that the corps lay in the floor upright.

775 And somme han dryve nayles in hir brayn

Whil that they slepte, and thus they han hem slayn.

Somme han hem yeve poysoun in hir drynke.

He spak moore harm than herte may bithynke,

And therwithal he knew of mo proverbes

780 Than in this world ther growen gras or herbes.

"Bet is," quod he, "thyn habitacioun

Be with a leon, or a foul dragoun,

Than with a womman usynge for to chyde."

"Bet is," quod he, "hye in the roof abyde

785 Than with an angry wyf doun in the hous,

They been so wikked and contrarious.

They haten that hir housbondes loveth ay."

He seyde, "a womman cast hir shame away

Whan she cast of hir smok," and forther mo,

790 "A fair womman, but she be chaast also,

Is lyk a goldryng in a sowes nose."

Who wolde leeve, or who wolde suppose

The wo that in myn herte was, and pyne?

And whan I saugh he wolde nevere fyne

795 To reden on this cursed book al nyght,

Al sodeynly thre leves have I plyght

Out of his book, right as he radde, and eke

I with my fest so took hym on the cheke,

That in oure fyr he ril bakward adoun.

800 And he up-stirte as dooth a wood leoun,

And with his fest he smoot me on the heed

That in the floor I lay, as I were deed.

And whan he saugh how stille that I lay,

He was agast, and wolde han fled his way,

While [their husband's] corpse lay face up on the floor.

775   *And some had nails driven into their brain*

While they slept, and thus had them killed.

Some had given them poison in their drink.

He spoke more evil than the heart can imagine.

And moreover, he knew of more proverbs

780   *Than there is grass or herbs growing in this world.*

"It is better," he said, "that your dwelling is [shared]

With a lion or a hideous dragon,",

"Than with a woman who is accustomed to scolding."

"It is better," he said, "to live high on the roof

785   *Than with an angry wife down in the house,*

They are so wicked and contrary,

They hate anything their husband loves, for sure."

He said, "a woman throws her shame away

When she takes off her undergarments," and furthermore,

790   *"An attractive woman, unless she is also chaste,*

Is like a gold ring in a pig's nose."

Who would imagine, or who would suppose

What grief and pain there was in my heart?

And when I saw he would never stop

795   *Reading this cursed book all night,*

Without warning, I pulled three leaves

Out of his book, as he read, and also

I struck him on the cheek with my fist,

[Such] that he fell backwards into our fire.

800   *And he stood up like an enraged lion,*

And with his fist he struck me on the head

That I lay on the floor, as if I was dead.

And when he saw how still I lay,

He was terrified, and would have run away,

805 Til atte laste out of my swogh I breyde.

'O, hastow slayn me, false theef,' I seyde,

'And for my land thus hastow mordred me?

Er I be deed, yet wol I kisse thee.'

And neer he cam and kneled faire adoun,

810 And seyde, 'Deere suster Alisoun,

As help me God, I shal thee nevere smyte.

That I have doon, it is thyself to wyte,

Foryeve it me, and that I thee biseke."

And yet eftsoones I hitte hym on the cheke,

815 And seyde, 'Theef, thus muchel am I wreke;

Now wol I dye, I may no lenger speke.'

But atte laste, with muchel care and wo,

We fille acorded by us selven two.

He yaf me al the bridel in myn hond,

820 To han the governance of hous and lond,

And of his tonge, and of his hond also,

And made hym brenne his book anon right tho.

And whan that I hadde geten unto me

By maistrie, al the soveraynetee,

825 And that he seyde, 'Myn owene trewe wyf,

Do as thee lust the terme of al thy lyf,

Keepe thyn honour, and keep eek myn estaat,' -

After that day we hadden never debaat.

God help me so, I was to hym as kynde

830 As any wyf from Denmark unto Ynde,

And also trewe, and so was he to me.

I prey to God, that sit in magestee,

So blesse his soule for his mercy deere.

Now wol I seye my tale, if ye wol heere.

53

805   *Until at last, I came out of my swoon,*

      'Oh, have you slain me, false thief?' I said,

      'And have you thus murdered me for my land?

      I want to kiss you before I die.'

      He came near to me and knelt down,

810   *And said: 'Dear sister Alison,*

      So help me God, I will never strike you [again];

      What I have done, it is you who is to blame,

      Forgive me for it, I beseech you!'

      And immediately after I hit him on the cheek,

815   *And said: 'Thief, by this much I am avenged!*

      Now I will die; I can no longer speak!'

      But at last, with much effort and sorrow,

      We two were reconciled between ourselves.

      He gave me all the bridle reins in my hand,

820   *To have control over the house and land;*

      And also over his tongue and his hand;

      And made him burn his book, right there and then!

      And when I had thereby gathered unto myself

      By mastery, all the sovereign [power],

825   *And that he said: 'My own true wife,*

      Do as you please for the rest of your life,

      Guard your own honour and also guard my social status' -

      After that day we never argued.

      God so help me, I was as kind to him

830   *As any wife from Denmark to India,*

      And also faithful, as he was to me.

      I pray to God, who sits in majesty,

      To bless his soul by His dear mercy.

      Now will I tell my tale, if you will listen.

835   The Frere lough whan he hadde herd al this.-

        "Now dame," quod he, "so have I joye or blis,

        This is a long preamble of a tale."

        And whan the Somonour herde the Frere gale,

        "Lo," quod the Somonour, "Goddes armes two,

840   A frere wol entremette hym everemo.

        Lo goode men, a flye and eek a frere

        Wol falle in every dyssh and eek mateere.

        What spekestow of preambulacioun?

        What, amble, or trotte, or pees, or go sit doun,

845   Thou lettest oure disport in this manere."

        "Ye, woltow so, sire Somonour?" quod the Frere,

        "Now by my feith, I shal er that I go

        Telle of a somonour swich a tale or two

        That alle the folk shal laughen in this place."

850   "Now elles, frere, I bishrewe thy face,"

        Quod this Somonour, "and I bishrewe me,

        But if I telle tales two or thre

        Of freres, er I come to Sidyngborne,

        That I shal make thyn herte for to morne,

855   For wel I woot thy pacience in gon."

        Oure Hooste cride, "Pees, and that anon!"

        And seyde, "lat the womman telle hire tale,

        Ye fare as folk that dronken were of ale.

        Do, dame, telle forth youre tale, and that is best."

860   "Al redy, sire," quod she, "right as yow lest,

        If I have licence of this worthy Frere."

        "Yis, dame," quod he, "tel forth, and I wol heere."

Heere endeth the Wyf of Bathe hir Prologe.

835   *The Friar laughed when he had heard all this.*

     'Now lady,' he said, 'so have I joy or bliss,

     This is a long introduction to a tale!'

     And when the Summoner heard the friar's interruption,

     'Lo,' said the Summoner, 'by God's two arms!

840   *A friar will always interfere,*

     Behold, good men, a housefly and also a friar

     Will fall into every dish and also into every subject.

     What can you say say about preambling?

     What! Amble or trot, hold your peace, or go sit down:

845   *In this way, you are stopping our fun.'*

     'Yes, is that what you say, sir Summoner?' said the Friar,

     Now by my faith I shall, before I go,

     Tell a tale or two about a Summoner such

     That all the folk in this place shall laugh.'

850   *Otherwise, Friar, I will curse your face,'*

     The Summoner said, 'and curse me,

     Unless I tell two or three tales

     Of friars, before I reach Sittingbourne,

     That will make your heart grieve,

855   *For I know very well that your patience is gone.'*

     Our host cried out, 'Peace, and that means now!'

     And said: 'Let the woman tell her tale,

     You act like people who are drunk with ale.

     Do, lady, tell your tale, and that is best.'

860   *'All ready, sir,' she said, 'as you desire,*

     If I have this worthy Friar's permission.'

     'Yes, lady,' he said, 'continue and I will listen.'

Here ends the Wife of Bath's Prologue

Heere bigynneth the Tale of the Wyf of Bathe.

In th'olde dayes of the Kyng Arthour,

Of which that Britons speken greet honour,

865   All was this land fulfild of fayerye.

The elf-queene, with hir joly compaignye,

Daunced ful ofte in many a grene mede.

This was the olde opinion, as I rede;

I speke of manye hundred yeres ago.

870   But now kan no man se none elves mo,

For now the grete charitee and prayeres

Of lymytours and othere hooly freres,

That serchen every lond and every streem,

As thikke as motes in the sonne-beem,

875   Blessynge halles, chambres, kichenes, boures,

Citees, burghes, castels, hye toures,

Thropes, bernes, shipnes, dayeryes,

This maketh that ther been no fayeryes.

For ther as wont to walken was an elf,

880   Ther walketh now the lymytour hymself

In undermeles and in morwenynges,

And seyth his matyns and his hooly thynges

As he gooth in his lymytacioun.

Wommen may go saufly up and doun.

885   In every bussh or under every tree

Ther is noon oother incubus but he,

And he ne wol doon hem but dishonour.

And so bifel it that this kyng Arthour

Hadde in his hous a lusty bacheler,

890   That on a day cam ridynge fro ryver;

And happed that, allone as she was born,

Here Begins the Wife of Bath's Tale

Now in the old days of King Arthur,

Of whom Britons speak with great honour,

865   *All this land was filled with elves and fairies.*

The elf-queen, with her jolly company,

Often danced on many a green meadow.

As I interpret, this was the opinion in olden times -

I speak of many hundred years ago.

870   *But now it is known that no man can see elves anymore.*

For now, the great charity and prayers

Of licensed friar-beggars and other holy friars,

Who search every land and every stream,

As thick as dust in a beam of sunlight,

875   *Blessing halls, rooms, kitchens, bedrooms,*

Cities, towns, castles, high towers,

Manors, barns, stables and dairies,

This causes that there are now no fairies.

For where an elf was accustomed to walk,

880   *The licensed friar-beggar now walks [instead]*

At midday and in the mornings,

Saying his matins and his prayers

As he goes around his licensed district.

Women may [now] go safely all the time,

885   *In every bush or under every tree*

There is no other evil spirit, but he,

And he would not do them any harm except dishonour.

And so it happened that this King Arthur

Had a lusty bachelor in his house,

890   *Who, one day, came riding from the falconry,*

And [it] happened that, as alone as [when] she was born,

He saugh a mayde walkynge hym biforn,

Of whiche mayde anon, maugree hir heed,

By verray force he rafte hir maydenhed;

895   For which oppressioun was swich clamour

And swich pursute unto the kyng Arthour,

That dampned was this knyght for to be deed,

By cours of lawe, and sholde han lost his heed -

Paraventure, swich was the statut tho -

900   But that the queene and othere ladyes mo

So longe preyeden the kyng of grace,

Til he his lyf hym graunted in the place,

And yaf hym to the queene al at hir wille,

To chese wheither she wolde hym save or spille.

905   The queene thanketh the kyng with al hir myght,

And after this thus spak she to the knyght,

Whan that she saugh hir tyme, upon a day,

"Thou standest yet," quod she, "in swich array

That of thy lyf yet hastow no suretee.

910   I grante thee lyf, if thou kanst tellen me

What thyng is it that wommen moost desiren.

Be war and keep thy nekke-boon from iren!

And if thou kanst nat tellen it anon,

Yet shal I yeve thee leve for to gon

915   A twelf-month and a day to seche and leere

An answere suffisant in this mateere;

And suretee wol I han, er that thou pace,

Thy body for to yelden in this place."

Wo was this knyght, and sorwefully he siketh;

920   But what! He may nat do al as hym liketh.

And at the laste he chees hym for to wende,

And come agayn right at the yeres ende,

He saw a maiden walking ahead of him,

From whom, immediately and despite of her resistance,

He took her virginity by sheer force.

895 *For which violation was there such an outcry*

And such an appeal to King Arthur,

That this knight was condemned to death,

[Who], by course of law, should have lost his head -

As, perhaps, such was then the law -

900 *But the queen and the other ladies as well*

Begged the king to show mercy,

Until he eventually agreed to spare his life right there,

And gave him to the queen, at her own will,

To choose whether she would save him or put to death.

905 *The queen thanked the king with all her heart,*

And after this, she then spoke to the knight,

One day, when she saw her chance,

'You stand yet,' she said, 'in such a poor state

That your life has no certainty.

910 *I will grant you life if you can tell me*

What thing it is that women most desire.

Be wise and save your neck from the iron [axe]!

And if you cannot tell it me straightaway,

Then I shall give you permission to be gone [for]

915 *A year and a day, to seek out and learn*

A satisfactory answer in this matter,

[But} I will have a guarantee before you leave,

That you will return here [at that time].'

This knight was grieved, and sighed sorrowfully,

920 *But he [knew] that he could not do as he pleased.*

And at last, he chose to depart,

And to return exactly at the year's end,

With swich answere as God wolde hym purveye;

And taketh his leve, and wendeth forth his weye.

925   He seketh every hous and every place

Where as he hopeth for to fynde grace

To lerne what thyng wommen loven moost;

But he ne koude arryven in no coost

Wher as he myghte fynde in this mateere

930   Two creatures accordynge in-feere.

Somme seyde, wommen loven best richesse,

Somme seyde honour, somme seyde jolynesse,

Somme riche array, somme seyden lust abedde,

And oftetyme to be wydwe and wedde.

935   Somme seyde, that oure hertes been moost esed

Whan that we been yflatered and yplesed.

He gooth ful ny the sothe, I wol nat lye,

A man shal wynne us best with flaterye;

And with attendance and with bisynesse

940   Been we ylymed, bothe moore and lesse.

And somme seyen, how that we loven best

For to be free, and do right as us lest,

And that no man repreve us of oure vice,

But seye that we be wise, and nothyng nyce.

945   For trewely, ther is noon of us alle,

If any wight wol clawe us on the galle,

That we nel kike; for he seith us sooth;

Assay, and he shal fynde it that so dooth.

For, be we never so vicious withinne,

950   We sol been holden wise, and clene of synne.

And somme seyn, that greet delit han we

For to been holden stable and eek secree,

And in o purpos stedefastly to dwelle,

With such an answer as God might provide for him,

And taking his leave, he went forth on his way.

925 *He sought out every house and every place*

Wherein he hoped to find the good fortune

To learn what women love the most;

But he could not arrive in any region

Where he found, in relation to this matter

930 *Two persons who agreed with each other.*

Some said that women loved wealth the best,

Some said, high reputation, some said gaiety,

Some [said], fine clothes, some said lust in bed,

And to be often widowed and re-married.

935 *Some said, that our hearts are most refreshed*

When we are flattered and pleased.

I will not lie, he got very close to the truth,

A man may win us best with flattery,

And with attention and with care

940 *Is how we are all caught, whether rich or poor.*

And some say, too, what we love the best [is]

To be free to do as we please,

And that no man reproaches us for our faults,

But to say that we are wise, and not foolish.

945 *For truly there is not one of us,*

If anyone shall rub us on a sore spot,

That will not kick back, since he tells the truth.

Try, and he shall find this will happen.

For, no matter how wicked we are on the inside,

950 *We want to be thought of as being wise and without sin.*

And some say that we take great delight

To be regarded as reliable and also as discrete,

And in one purpose to continue steadfastly,

And nat biwreye thyng that men us telle.

955   But that tale is nat worth a rake-stele,

Pardee, we wommen konne no thyng hele.

Witnesse on Myda, - wol ye heere the tale?

Ovyde, amonges othere thynges smale,

Seyde Myda hadde under his longe heres

960   Growynge upon his heed two asses eres,

The whiche vice he hydde, as he best myghte,

Ful subtilly from every mannes sighte,

That, save his wyf, ther wiste of it namo.

He loved hire moost and trusted hir also;

965   He preyede hire, that to no creature

She sholde tellen of his disfigure.

She swoor him nay, for al this world to wynne,

She nolde do that vileynye or synne,

To make hir housbonde han so foul a name.

970   She nolde nat telle it for hir owene shame.

But nathelees, hir thoughte that she dyde,

That she so longe sholde a conseil hyde;

Hir thoughte it swal so soore aboute hir herte

That nedely som word hir moste asterte;

975   And sith she dorste telle it to no man,

Doun to a mareys faste by she ran,

Til she cam there, hir herte was a fyre,

And as a bitore bombleth in the myre,

She leyde hir mouth unto the water doun:

980   "Biwreye me nat, thou water, with thy soun,"

Quod she, "to thee I telle it and namo,

Myn housbonde hath longe asses erys two!

Now is myn herte al hool, now is it oute.

I myghte no lenger kepe it, out of doute."

63

And not betray anything that men may tell us.

955 *But that tale is not worth a rake's handle,*

By God, we women cannot hide anything.

Witness King Midas. Do you want to hear the tale?

Ovid, among other small matters,

Said Midas had beneath his long hair

960 *Two ass's ears growing on his head,*

A defect which he hid, as best as he could,

Very skilfully from everyone's sight,

That, except his wife, there was no-one else who knew about it.

He loved her greatly, and also trusted her;

965 *And entreated her that, to no creature*

Would she tell about his disfigurement.

She swore to him that, not even to gain the whole world,

Would she commit that dishonour or sin,

To make her husband have such a bad reputation.

970 *Nor would she tell it due to her own deep shame.*

Nevertheless, she thought she would die,

Having to keep a secret for so long;

She thought that it swelled so sorely around her heart

That some word must surely slip from her mouth -

975 *And since she dared to tell no man,*

She ran down to a nearby marsh,

Her heart was on fire until she arrived there,

And like a bittern booming in the muddy reed beds,

She lowered her mouth down to the water:

980 *'Betray me not, you water, with your sound,'*

She said, 'I tell it to none else but you,

My husband has two long asses' ears!

Now that is out, my heart is now at ease.

Without doubt, I could no longer keep it [secret].'

985   Heere may ye se, thogh we a tyme abyde,

     Yet out it moot, we kan no conseil hyde.

     The remenant of the tale, if ye wol heere,

     Redeth Ovyde, and ther ye may it leere.

     This knyght, of which my tale is specially,

990   Whan that he saugh he myghte nat come therby,

     This is to seye, what wommen love moost,

     Withinne his brest ful sorweful was the goost.

     But hoom he gooth, he myghte nat sojourne;

     The day was come that homward moste he tourne.

995   And in his wey it happed hym to ryde,

     In al this care under a forest syde,

     Wher as he saugh upon a daunce go

     Of ladyes foure and twenty, and yet mo;

     Toward the whiche daunce he drow ful yerne,

1000   In hope that som wysdom sholde he lerne.

     But certeinly, er he came fully there,

     Vanysshed was this daunce, he nyste where.

     No creature saugh he that bar lyf,

     Save on the grene he saugh sittynge a wyf -

1005   A fouler wight ther may no man devyse.

     Agayn the knyght this olde wyf gan ryse,

     And seyde, "Sire knyght, heer forth ne lith no wey.

     Tel me what that ye seken, by your fey!

     Paraventure it may the bettre be,

1010   Thise olde folk kan muchel thyng," quod she.

     "My leeve mooder," quod this knyght, "certeyn

     I nam but deed, but if that I kan seyn

     What thyng it is, that wommen moost desire.

     Koude ye me wisse, I wolde wel quite youre hire."

1015   "Plight me thy trouthe, heere in myn hand," quod she,

985 *Here may you see, though we may wait for a while,*

Yet it must come out, we do not know how to hide any secret.

If you want to hear the rest of this tale,

Read Ovid, and you may learn about it there.

This knight, who is the subject of my tale,

990 *When he saw that he might not come by it,*

That is to say, the thing that women love most,

He had a very sorrowful spirit within his breast.

But could not delay any longer from going home

[Since] the day had come when he must turn homeward.

995 *And on his way he happened to ride,*

With all care under a forest's edge,

Where he saw a dance going on

Of twenty-four ladies, maybe more,

Towards which dance he turned eagerly,

1000 *In hope that he should learn some wisdom.*

But truly, before he fully arrived there,

The dancers all vanished, he knew not where.

He saw no creature that showed sign of life,

Except an old wife sitting in a field -

1005 *No man could imagine an uglier person.*

Before the knight arrived, this old wife arose,

And said: 'Sir knight, from here on there is no path.

By your faith! Tell me what thing you are seeking.

Perhaps it would be for the better;

1010 *[Since] these old folk know many things,' she said.*

'My dear mother,' said this knight, 'It is certain that

I am as good as dead, unless I know to say

What thing it is that women desire most.

Could you guide me, I will repay you well.'

1015 *'Pledge your word, here in my hand,' she said,*

"The nexte thyng that I requere thee,

Thou shalt it do, if it lye in thy myght,

And I wol telle it yow, er it be nyght."

"Have heer my trouthe," quod the knyght, "I grante."

1020 "Thanne," quod she, "I dar me wel avante

Thy lyf is sauf; for I wol stonde therby,

Upon my lyf, the queene wol seye as I.

Lat se which is the proudeste of hem alle,

That wereth on a coverchief or a calle,

1025 That dar seye nay of that I shal thee teche.

Lat us go forth withouten lenger speche."

Tho rowned she a pistel in his ere,

And bad hym to be glad and have no fere.

Whan they be comen to the court, this knyght

1030 Seyde he had holde his day, as he hadde hight,

And redy was his answere, as he sayde.

Ful many a noble wyf, and many a mayde,

And many a wydwe, for that they been wise,

The queene hirself sittynge as a justise,

1035 Assembled been, his answere for to heere;

And afterward this knyght was bode appeere.

To every wight comanded was silence,

And that the knyght sholde telle in audience

What thyng that worldly wommen loven best.

1040 This knyght ne stood nat stille as doth a best,

But ot his questioun anon answerde

With manly voys, that al the court it herde:

"My lige lady, generally," quod he,

"Wommen desiren to have sovereynetee

1045 As wel over hir housbond as hir love,

And for to been in maistrie hym above.

67

'The next thing that I require from you,

'You shall do it, if it lies within your power,

And I will answer you, before it is night.'

'Have my pledge here,' said the knight. 'I grant it [to you].'

1020 *'Then,' she said, 'of this I make my boast*

Your life is safe; for I will stand thereby,

Upon my life, the queen will say as I.

Let us see which is the proudest of them all,

That wears her kerchief or a hairnet,

1025 *That dares say 'no' to what I shall teach you.*

Let us now go without further words.'

Then, she whispered a message in his ear,

And told him to be happy and have no fear.

When they arrived at the court, this knight

1030 *Said he had kept his appointment, as he had promised,*

And said he was ready with his answer.

Many noble wives and many maidens,

And many widows, because they be so wise,

[With] the queen herself sitting as judge,

1035 *Were assembled to hear his answer.*

And then the knight was summoned to appear.

Every person was commanded to be silent,

And that the knight should tell the audience

What thing that worldly women love best.

1040 *This knight did not stand like a dumb beast,*

But answered this question immediately

With a manly voice, so that the entire court heard it:

'My liege lady, across the world,' he said,

'Women desire to have sovereignty

1045 *Over both their husband as well as over their love,*

And to have mastery over him.

This is youre mooste desir, thogh ye me kille.

Dooth as yow list, I am heer at youre wille."

In al the court ne was ther wyf, ne mayde,

1050 Ne wydwe, that contraried that he sayde,

But seyden he was worthy han his lyf.

And with that word up stirte the olde wyf,

Which that the knyght saugh sittynge in the grene.

"Mercy," quod she, "my sovereyn lady queene,

1055 Er that youre court departe, do me right.

I taughte this answere unto the knyght,

For which he plighte me his trouthe there,

The firste thyng I wolde of hym requere,

He wolde it do, if it lay in his myght.

1060 Bifor the court thanne preye I thee, sir knyght,"

Quod she, "that thou me take unto thy wyf,

For wel thou woost that I have kept thy lyf.

If I seye fals, sey nay, upon thy fey!"

This knyght answerde, "Allas and weylawey!

1065 I woot right wel that swich was my biheste!

For Goddes love, as chees a newe requeste!

Taak al my good, and lat my body go!"

"Nay, thanne," quod she, "I shrewe us bothe two!

For thogh that I be foul, and oold, and poore,

1070 I nolde for al the metal, ne for oore,

That under erthe is grave, or lith above,

But if thy wyf I were, and eek thy love."

"My love?" quod he, "nay, my dampnacioun!

Allas, that any of my nacioun

1075 Sholde evere so foule disparaged be!"

But al for noght, the ende is this, that he

Constreyned was, he nedes moste hir wedde;

This is your greatest desire, though you may kill me.

Do as you wish, I am here subject to your will.'

In all the court there was not one wife, or maiden,

1050 *Or widow who contradicted what he had said,*

But all said, he was worthy to have his life.

And with that word up stood the old wife,

Whom he had seen sitting in the field.

'Mercy,' she cried, 'my sovereign lady queen!

1055 *Before your court departs, give me justice.*

[It was} I who taught this answer to the knight,

For which he pledged his word to me, out there,

The first thing I would require of him,

He would do it, if it lay in his power.

1060 *Before the court, then, ask I you, sir knight,'*

She said, 'that you will take me as your wife,

For you know very well that I have saved your life.

If I speak falsely, say 'no', upon your faith!'

This knight replied: 'Alas and woe!

1065 *I know full well that I made such a promise!*

[But] for God's love, choose a new request!

Take all my wealth and let my body go [free].'

'No, then,' said she, 'I curse us both!

For though I may be disgusting and old and poor,

1070 *I will not, for all the metal, nor for the ore,*

That is buried under the earth, or lies above it,

[Be] anything except your wife and your true love.'

'My love?' he said, 'no, my damnation!

Alas! that anyone of my station

1075 *Should ever be so foully dishonoured!'*

But all this was for nothing, the conclusion is that he

Was compelled by necessity, and must wed her

And taketh his olde wyf, and gooth to bedde.

Now wolden som men seye, paraventure,

1080 That for my necligence I do no cure

To tellen yow the joye and al th'array,

That at the feeste was that ilke day;

To whiche thyng shortly answere I shal:

I seye, ther nas no joye ne feeste at al;

1085 Ther nas but hevynesse and muche sorwe.

For prively he wedde hir on a morwe,

And al day after hidde hym as an owle,

So wo was hym, his wyf looked so foule.

Greet was the wo the knyght hadde in his thoght,

1090 Whan he was with his wyf abedde ybroght;

He walweth and he turneth to and fro.

His olde wyf lay smylynge everemo,

And seyde, "O deere housbonde, benedicitee,

Fareth every knyght thus with his wyf, as ye?

1095 Is this the lawe of Kyng Arthures hous?

Is every knyght of his so dangerous?

I am youre owene love and youre wyf;

I am she which that saved hath youre lyf.

And certes, yet dide I yow nevere unright;

1100 Why fare ye thus with me this firste nyght?

Ye faren lyk a man had lost his wit.

What is my gilt? For Goddes love, tel it,

And it shal been amended, if I may."

"Amended," quod this knyght, "allas! nay! nay!

1105 It wol nat been amended nevere mo;

Thou art so loothly and so oold also,

And therto comen of so lough a kynde,

That litel wonder is thogh I walwe and wynde.

71

And take his old wife and go to bed.

Now, perhaps, some men might say,

1080   *That, I am negligent in not taking care*

To tell you about the joy and all the preparations,

Which were seen at the celebrations that same day,

To this thing, I shall give you a brief answer:

I say, there was no joy or feast at all

1085   *There was only heaviness [of heart] and great sorrow.*

For he wedded her in private the next morning,

And for all day afterwards, he hid himself away like an owl,

As he was sorrowful that his wife looked so ugly.

The knight's thoughts were full of great woe,

1090   *When he was brought to bed with his wife;*

He tossed and turned backwards and forwards.

His old wife lay there, smiling continuously,

And said: 'O my dear husband, God bless!

Does every knight conduct himself thus with his wife, as you?

1095   *Is this the custom in King Arthur's house?*

Are knights of his all so disdainful?

I am your own true love and your wife:

I am she who has saved your very life.

And truly, I have never done you any wrong;

1100   *[So] why behave like this with me on the first night?*

You act like a man who has lost his mind.

What is my crime? For the love of God tell it to me,

And it shall be corrected, if I can.'

'Corrected,' said this knight, 'Alas, nay, nay!

1105   *It will not be corrected for ever more;*

You are so loathsome, and also so old,

And come from such a low ancestry,

It is little wonder that I toss and turn.

So wolde God, myn herte wolde breste!"

1110 "Is this," quod she, "the cause of youre unreste?"

"Ye certeinly," quod he, "no wonder is!"

"Now, sire," quod she, "I koude amende al this,

If that me liste, er it were dayes thre,

So wel ye myghte bere yow unto me.

1115 But for ye speken of swich gentillesse

As is descended out of old richesse,

That therfore sholden ye be gentil men,

Swich arrogance nis nat worth an hen.

Looke who that is moost vertuous alway,

1120 Pryvee and apert, and moost entendeth ay

To do the gentil dedes that he kan,

Taak hym for the grettest gentil man.

Crist wole we clayme of hym oure gentillesse,

Nat of oure eldres for hire old richesse.

1125 For thogh they yeve us al hir heritage,

For which we clayme to been of heigh parage,

Yet may they nat biquethe, for no thyng

To noon of us hir vertuous lyvyng,

That made hem gentil men ycalled be,

1130 And bad us folwen hem in swich degree.

Wel kan the wise poete of Florence,

That highte Dant, speken in this sentence.

Lo in swich maner rym is Dantes tale:

`Ful selde upriseth by his branches smale

1135 Prowesse of man, for God of his goodnesse,

Wole, that of hym we clayme oure gentillesse.'

For of oure eldres may we no thyng clayme

But temporel thyng, that man may hurte and mayme.

Eek every wight woot this as wel as I,

So would that God would make my heart burst!'

1110 *'Is this,' she said, 'the cause of your distress?'*

'Yes, truly,' he said, 'and it is no wonder!'

'Now, sir,' she said, 'I could correct all this,

If I wished, before three days have passed,

Provided that you behave well to me.

1115 *'But as you speak about such [high] nobility*

That is descended from old wealth,

You should therefore be a noble man,

[However] such arrogance is worthless.

Look at who is always the most virtuous,

1120 *In private or public, and [who] tries most hard*

To do the noble deeds that he knows,

Take him to be the greatest gentleman.

Christ wills us to claim our nobility from Him,

Not from our ancestors for their old wealth.

1125 *For although they give us all their heritage,*

From which we claim to be of high descent,

Yet they may not bequeath any

Of their virtues to any of us,

That made them be called noble gentlemen,

1130 *And ordered us follow them in every such way.*

Well knows that wise poet from Florence,

Who is called Dante, speaks on this matter.

Look, Dante's tale says in this manner of rhyme

"It is seldom that, [any] further along a family tree,

1135 *Will a man's excellence extend; for God, in his goodness.*

Wishes us to claim our nobility from Him",

Since, from our ancestors, we can claim nothing

But worldly things, with which man may hurt and injure.

Also, every person knows this as well as I,

1140 If gentillesse were planted natureelly

Unto a certeyn lynage doun the lyne,

Pryvee nor apert, thanne wolde they nevere fyne

To doon of gentillesse the faire office,

They myghte do no vileynye or vice.

1145 Taak fyr, and ber it in the derkeste hous

Bitwix this and the mount of Kaukasous,

And lat men shette the dores and go thenne;

Yet wole the fyr as faire lye and brenne

As twenty thousand men myghte it biholde;

1150 His office natureel ay wol it holde,

Up peril of my lyf, til that it dye.

Heere may ye se wel, how that genterye

Is nat annexed to possessioun,

Sith folk ne doon hir operacioun

1155 Alwey, as dooth the fyr, lo, in his kynde.

For God it woot, men may wel often fynde

A lordes sone do shame and vileynye,

And he that wole han pris of his gentrye,

For he was boren of a gentil hous,

1160 And hadde hise eldres noble and vertuous,

And nel hym-selven do no gentil dedis,

Ne folwen his gentil auncestre that deed is,

He nys nat gentil, be he duc or erl;

For vileyns synful dedes make a cherl.

1165 For gentillesse nys but renomee

Of thyne auncestres for hire heigh bountee,

Which is a strange thyng to thy persone.

Thy gentillesse cometh fro God allone.

Thanne comth oure verray gentillesse of grace,

1170   It was no thyng biquethe us with oure place.

1140   *That if nobility was implanted by nature*

Into the line of a particular family,

They would never refrain, in public or private,

From performing their duties of nobility,

[That] they would never commit dishonour or sin.

1145   *Take fire and carry it into the darkest house*

Between here and the Mount of Caucasus,

And let men shut their doors and go thenceforth [away].

Yet the fire will [continue to] blaze and burn

As if twenty thousand men were watching,

1150   *It will always perform its natural function,*

I swear upon my life, until it dies.

Here you can see that nobility

Is not related to possessions,

Since folk do not behave

1155   *According to nature, as the fire always does.*

For God knows, men may very often find

A lord's son committing shame and dishonour,

And he that praises his own nobility,

Because of being born to some noble house,

1160   *And had noble and virtuous ancestors,*

And will do none of those noble deeds himself,

Nor follow [the example] of his deceased noble ancestors,

He is not noble, [whether] he be a duke or an earl;

For villainous, sinful deeds make a man a peasant.

1165   *Nobility is nothing but renown*

Of your ancestors for their great virtue,

Which is an alien thing to your person.

Your nobility comes from God alone.

Thence comes our true nobility by [His] grace,

1170   *It was not bequeathed to us with our title or rank.*

Thenketh hou noble, as seith Valerius,

Was thilke Tullius Hostillius,

That out of poverte roos to heigh noblesse.

Reedeth Senek, and redeth eek Boece,

1175 Ther shul ye seen expres that it no drede is,

That he is gentil that dooth gentil dedis.

And therfore, leeve housbonde, I thus conclude:

Al were it that myne auncestres weren rude,

Yet may the hye God, and so hope I,

1180 Grante me grace to lyven vertuously.

Thanne am I gentil whan that I bigynne

To lyven vertuously, and weyve synne.

And ther as ye of poverte me repreeve,

The hye God, on whom that we bileeve,

1185 In wilful poverte chees to lyve his lyf.

And certes every man, mayden or wyf,

May understonde that Jesus, hevene kyng,

Ne wolde nat chesen vicious lyvyng.

Glad poverte is an honeste thyng, certeyn,

1190 This wole Senec and othere clerkes seyn.

Who so that halt hym payd of his poverte,

I holde hym riche, al hadde he nat a sherte.

He that coveiteth is a povre wight,

For he wolde han that is nat in his myght;

1195 But he that noght hath, ne coveiteth have,

Is riche, although ye holde hym but a knave.

Verray poverte, it syngeth proprely;

Juvenal seith of poverte myrily:

`The povre man, whan he goth by the weye,

1200 Bifore the theves he may synge and pleye.'

Poverte is hateful good, and, as I gesse,

Think how noble, as Valerius said,

Was that same Tullius Hostilius,

Who rose out of poverty to high nobility.

Read Seneca, and also read Boethius,

1175 *There, you shall see clearly, there is no doubt,*

That he is noble who does noble deeds.

And therefore, dear husband, I thus conclude:

That although my ancestors were of low birth,

So I hope that yet may the high God,

1180 *Grant me the favour to live virtuously.*

Then I am noble when I begin

To live virtuously, and eschew sin.

And whereas you reproach me for my poverty,

The high God, in whom we believe,

1185 *Chose freely to live his life in poverty.*

And certainly, every man, or maiden, or wife,

May understand that Jesus, Heaven's king,

Would not have chosen a wicked way of living.

Truly, cheerful poverty is an honest thing,

1190 *Which Seneca and other scholars say.*

Whosoever is satisfied with his poverty,

I consider him to be rich, although he has not [even] a shirt.

He who covets is a poor person,

For he would have that which is not in his power

1195 *But he that has nothing, nor desires to have [anything],*

Is rich, even though you consider him as only a servant.

True poverty, sings its own song;

Juvenal merrily speaks about poverty:

"The poor man, when he goes along the way,

1200 *Before the robbers he can sing and play."*

Poverty is a horrible good, and, as I guess,

A ful greet bryngere out of bisynesse;

A greet amender eek of sapience

To hym that taketh it in pacience.

1205 Poverte is this, although it seme alenge,

Possessioun, that no wight wol chalenge.

Poverte ful ofte, whan a man is lowe,

Maketh his God and eek hymself to knowe.

Poverte a spectacle is, as thynketh me,

1210 Thurgh which he may hise verray freendes see.

And therfore, sire, syn that I noght yow greve,

Of my poverte namoore ye me repreve.

Now sire, of elde ye repreve me,

And certes, sire, thogh noon auctoritee

1215 Were in no book, ye gentils of honour

Seyn, that men sholde an oold wight doon favour,

And clepe hym fader for youre gentillesse;

And auctours shal I fynden, as I gesse.

Now, ther ye seye that I am foul and old,

1220 Than drede you noght to been a cokewold;

For filthe and eelde, al so moot I thee,

Been grete wardeyns upon chastitee;

But nathelees, syn I knowe youre delit,

I shal fulfille youre worldly appetit."

1225 "Chese now," quod she, "oon of thise thynges tweye:

To han me foul and old til that I deye,

And be to yow a trewe humble wyf,

And nevere yow displese in al my lyf;

Or elles ye wol han me yong and fair,

1230 And take youre aventure of the repair

That shal be to youre hous, by cause of me,

Or in som oother place may wel be.

It is a great remover of concerns,

And is also great improver of wisdom

For him that takes it in with patience.

1205   *Poverty is this, although it seems wretched,*

It is a possession that no other person wants.

When a man is [so] humbled, poverty very often,

Makes him know his God and also himself.

It seems to me that poverty is an eye-glass,

1210   *Through which a man may see his true friends.*

And therefore, sir, since I have not brought you grief,

You should no longer reproach me for my poverty.

Now, sir, you reproach me for being old -

And truly, sir, although there is no authority

1215   *In any book, you gentlemen of honour*

Say that men should show respect to the aged,

And call him father, due to your nobility;

I believe I could find authors [who agree].

Now since you say that I am ugly and old,

1220   *There is no fear of having an adulterous wife;*

For, may I prosper, foulness and old age,

Are great protectors of chastity.

But, nevertheless, since I know your delight,

I shall satisfy your worldly appetite.'

1225   *'Choose, now,' she said, 'one of these two things:*

To have me ugly and old until I die,

And to be your true and humble wife,

And never to anger you for all my life;

Or else to have me young and beautiful,

1230   *And take your chance with the visits*

There shall be to your house, because of me,

Or in some other place, as well may be.'

Now chese yourselven wheither that yow liketh."

This knyght avyseth hym and sore siketh,

1235 But atte laste, he seyde in this manere:

"My lady and my love, and wyf so deere,

I put me in youre wise governance.

Cheseth yourself, which may be moost plesance

And moost honour to yow and me also.

1240 I do no fors the wheither of the two;

For, as yow liketh, it suffiseth me."

"Thanne have I gete of yow maistrie," quod she,

"Syn I may chese and governe as me lest?"

"Ye, certes, wyf," quod he, "I holde it best."

1245 "Kys me," quod she, "we be no lenger wrothe,

For, by my trouthe, I wol be to yow bothe!

This is to seyn, ye, bothe fair and good.

I prey to God that I moote sterven wood

But I to yow be al so good and trewe

1250 As evere was wyf, syn that the world was newe.

And but I be to-morn as fair to seene

As any lady, emperice, or queene,

That is bitwixe the est and eke the west,

Dooth with my lyf and deth right as yow lest.

1255 Cast up the curtyn, looke how that it is."

And whan the knyght saugh verraily al this,

That she so fair was, and so yong therto,

For joye he hente hire in hise armes two.

His herte bathed in a bath of blisse,

1260 A thousand tyme a-rewe he gan hir kisse,

And she obeyed hym in every thyng

That myghte doon hym plesance or likyng.

And thus they lyve unto hir lyves ende

In parfit joye;-and Jesu Crist us sende

Now choose whichever pleases you.'

This knight considered, and sighed bitterly,

1235 *But at last, he spoke in this manner,*

'My lady and my love, and wife so dear,

I put myself in your wise control.

Choose yourself whichever is the most pleasing

And [brings] the most honour to you, and to me also.

1240 *I do not care which of these two,*

For if you like it, that is enough for me.'

'Then I have gained mastery over you,' she said,

'Since may I choose and govern as I wish?'

'Yes, truly, wife,' he said, 'I consider that is best.'

1245 *'Kiss me,' she said, 'we shall no longer be angry,*

For by my truth, I will be both to you!

That is to say, I will be both beautiful and good.

I pray to God that I will die insane

Unless I am not as good and true to you

1250 *As ever a was wife since the world began.*

And unless, by tomorrow morning, I am as beautiful to see

As any lady, empress, or queen,

That is, between the [furthest] east and also the [furthest] west,

Do with my life and death as you please.

1255 *Lift the curtain and see how it is.'*

And when the knight truly saw all this,

That she was so very beautiful, and moreover so young,

With joy he embraced her in his two arms.

His heart bathed in a blissful bath,

1260 *He kissed her a thousand times in a row,*

And she obeyed him in everything

That might give him pleasure or sexual enjoyment.

And thus they lived to the end of their lives

In perfect joy; and Jesus Christ to send us

1265   Housbondes meeke, yonge, fressh abedde,
And grace t'overbyde hem that we wedde;
And eek I praye Jesu shorte hir lyves
That nat wol be governed by hir wyves;
And olde and angry nygardes of dispence,
1270   God sende hem soone verray pestilence!

Heere endeth the Wyves Tale of Bathe.

1265　*Husbands that are meek, young and full of vigour in bed,*

　　　And have the good luck to outlive those whom we wed,

　　　And I also pray Jesus to cut short the lives

　　　Of those who will not be governed by their wives.

　　　And to old and angry misers with their money,

1270　*May God soon send them the true plague!*

Here ends the Wife of Bath's Tale.

55399844R00055